MW01075551

A Tale of Two Tabbies

by

Kathi Daley

This book is a work of fiction. Names, characters, places, and incidents either are products of the author's imagination or are used fictitiously. Any resemblance to actual events or locales or persons, living or dead, is entirely coincidental.

Copyright © 2016 by Katherine Daley

Version 1.0

All rights reserved, including the right of reproduction in whole or in part in any form.

This book is dedicated to the readers who pitch in and offer comments and suggestions when I ask for input. It is also dedicated to the fans who help to provide technical information when needed, including a friend who is retired military who did not want to be mentioned.

I also want to thank the very talented Jessica Fischer for the cover art.

I so appreciate Bruce Curran, who is always ready and willing to answer my cyber questions.

And, of course, thanks to the readers and bloggers in my life, who make doing what I do possible.

Thank you to Randy Ladenheim-Gil for the editing.

Special thanks to Nancy Farris, Pamela Curran, Vivian Shane, Joyce Aiken, Teri Fish, and Pam Woodfield for submitting recipes.

And finally I want to thank my sister Christy for always lending an ear and my husband Ken for allowing me time to write by taking care of everything else.

Books by Kathi Daley

Come for the murder, stay for the romance.

Zoe Donovan Cozy Mystery:

Halloween Hijinks
The Trouble With Turkeys
Christmas Crazy
Cupid's Curse
Big Bunny Bump-off
Beach Blanket Barbie
Maui Madness
Derby Divas
Haunted Hamlet
Turkeys, Tuxes, and Tabbies
Christmas Cozy
Alaskan Alliance
Matrimony Meltdown
Soul Surrender
Heavenly Honeymoon
Hopscotch Homicide
Ghostly Graveyard
Santa Sleuth
Shamrock Shenanigans

Zimmerman Academy Shorts

The New Normal
New Beginnings – *March 2016*

Paradise Lake Cozy Mystery:

Pumpkins in Paradise
Snowmen in Paradise
Bikinis in Paradise
Christmas in Paradise
Puppies in Paradise
Halloween in Paradise

Whales and Tails Cozy Mystery:

Romeow and Juliet
The Mad Catter
Grimm's Furry Tail
Much Ado About Felines
Legend of Tabby Hollow
Cat of Christmas Past
A Tale of Two Tabbies

Sand and Sea Hawaiian Mystery

Murder at Dolphin Bay – *March 2016*

Seacliff High Mystery:

The Secret
The Curse
The Relic
The Conspiracy
The Grudge

Road to Christmas Romance:

Road to Christmas Past

Chapter 1

Wednesday, April 20

Love in its purest form is selfless and eternal. It endures all things and exists independently of the opinion of others. Love that is born in the soul and lives in the heart, will thrive and prosper in spite of the challenges it must face and the hardships it must endure.

I really don't know why I was surprised to find Theresa Lively's cat locked in the confessional of a deserted church in the middle of a rainstorm. My life has been so bizarre as of late that I really should expect that almost anything that *could* happen *will* happen. Of course the fact that Theresa hadn't shown up for choir practice and, as far as I knew, wasn't even on the premises, did lend an air of mystery to the event that couldn't quite be explained.

"Did you find the sheet music we're looking for?" my boyfriend and co-choir director Cody West asked after walking in through the door connecting the main body of the church with the offices and classrooms. I imagine he must have come looking for me after I failed to return to the choir room in a reasonable amount of time.

"No, but I did find Sydney."

"Sydney?"

I reached into confessional number one and picked up the reddish orange cat that was still cowering in the corner. I gently cuddled him to my chest before taking a step back so Cody could see what it was I was holding.

"Oh, Sydney," Cody said as he recognized the cat. "I take it Theresa is around as well?"

"I haven't seen her."

Cody frowned. I watched his face as he worked through the same thought I'd been having since I'd discovered that Sydney was responsible for the strange scratching sound I'd heard.

"We'd better call Finn," Cody suggested.

Ryan Finnegan, Finn for short, was the resident deputy of Madrona Island and my older sister Siobhan's current boyfriend and ex-fiancé.

"Finn and Siobhan are planning to go out to dinner to celebrate some sort of an anniversary. I'm honestly not sure what sort, but Siobhan bought a new dress and everything. I hate to disturb them over a cat locked in a confessional. What if Sydney was simply locked up by some kids pulling a prank? Theresa does live just a block from the church. It's totally possible Sydney was catting around the neighborhood when he was picked up and brought to the church."

"I guess you have a point."

I looked around the empty room as I tried to decide what to do. I'd been attending St. Patrick's Catholic Church my entire life. The rows of wooden pews, the sturdy tile floor, and the beautiful stained-glass windows filled me with a sense of comfort and familiarity. As far as I could tell, nothing had been disturbed and there didn't appear to be any signs of a struggle. Yes, it was odd that Sydney had been locked up, but I really did hate to disrupt Siobhan's evening and we really didn't have any reason to suspect Theresa was in any sort of immediate danger.

"Rehearsal is almost over. The parents should begin arriving any time. We'll take Sydney home after the kids are picked up, and if we find anything to suggest foul play we'll call Finn then," I said.

"Yeah, I guess that makes sense. I'm going to try calling Theresa's house line again just in case she's home. She is somewhat absentminded and she's missed rehearsal before, so the fact that she isn't here shouldn't really be cause for alarm."

"I'm sure it will be fine. I'll head back to the choir room. It's not a good idea to leave the kids alone too long."

When my mother first suggested that I take over as director for the children's choir I wasn't sure I wanted to do it. I have a busy life and it seemed like it would be something of a hassle to fit one more thing into my schedule. I dragged my feet when it came to making a commitment, but as it turned out, directing the choir has been both fun and rewarding. If I had to do it over again I would leap at the chance to work with the twenty-four kids between the ages of six and fourteen who make up the eclectic and talented group.

"What are you doing with Mrs. Lively's cat Ms. Cait?" Annabelle Sawyer asked when I returned to the room.

"I found him in the church," I answered. "I'll take him home if Mrs. Lively doesn't show up. How about we practice the new number Cody added for Sunday's performance before your parents arrive to pick you up?"

"I don't know why you bother. Everyone but me is off key," Annabelle complained.

"It sounded good to me when we practiced it last week," I countered. Annabelle had a beautiful voice, but she was severely lacking in the personality department. As far as she was concerned, no one other than herself could carry a tune, and she was sure to let everyone know it. Repeatedly.

"That's because you're tone death. Trust me, it was bad."

"I'm not tone *deaf*," I defended myself. "And it wasn't bad. Let's take it from the top. And Annabelle, please remember that everyone has a differing talent level and rigid adherence to a standard only you can meet doesn't make for a choir."

"I just think I should sing the solos and everyone else should hum in the background or something."

I rolled my eyes. The girl really was full of herself.

"What about Miranda?" Serenity asked.

Miranda Madison was a new member of the choir who had joined us for the very first time that day. She'd moved to the island to live with her grandmother after her parents were killed in a plane crash. So far she hadn't said a word; her grandmother had told me that she hadn't said a word to anyone since her parents' death. I thought it odd that her grandmother would sign her up for the choir considering she didn't speak, but when I asked her about that she'd shared with me that prior to the accident Miranda had loved to sing and she hoped being around music would ease her from the shell she'd been living in for the past couple of months.

I watched as Sydney approached Miranda. I couldn't be certain, but I could swear I noticed a small smile on Miranda's face when the cat jumped into her lap. Miranda didn't say a word, but I did see her arms tighten just slightly around the furry orange body of the large cat.

"Miranda is going to keep an eye on Sydney for me," I informed the others. "Let's take it from the top, and this time remember the new bridge we've been practicing."

I watched Miranda out of the corner of my eye as I led the kids through the number. I couldn't hear anything, but her lips were moving, and it appeared she was talking to Sydney, who, oddly enough, seemed to be listening intently. I wasn't certain if Miranda's grandmother's living arrangement would allow for a pet, but based on the light in Miranda's eyes, I was definitely going to suggest she come by the cat sanctuary to take a look at the cats and kittens currently available for adoption.

"I'll go get the car and meet you at the door," Cody offered once the last of the members of the St. Patrick's Catholic Church Children's Choir had been picked up. "No use both of us getting wet."

"I need to run down the hall to pick up some notes Father Kilian wanted me to bring to the planning meeting for the community dinner. He said he has to go out of town for a few days and is going to miss the meeting, but he wanted to be sure his ideas were presented."

"Okay. I'll take Sydney with me. I'll be waiting for you out front."

I quickly made my way down the hallway where several offices were located. I let my way into Father Kilian's and turned on the light. Just as he'd instructed, there was a medium-size envelope on his desk, which he'd assured me would contain his notes. When I reached for the envelope I noticed that a book of some sort had fallen to the floor. I picked it up and looked at it. It was a high school yearbook. Based on the year indicated on the cover, I was willing to bet it was Father Kilian's own high school yearbook.

I opened the book and looked inside. The name Michael Kilian was written in a neat script across the top of the first page. I'd recently learned that Father Kilian had not only grown up on the island but had graduated from Madrona High School, where he'd dated my Aunt Maggie some forty odd years ago when they were both teenagers. While there were those around who probably remembered that fact, I was pretty sure I was the only one who knew how close he'd been to shunning his calling to the priesthood in order to run away with the love of his life.

Maggie never did say what it was that had changed his mind, but he'd ended up accepting the calling he was destined for, and Maggie had been living out her life alone. I suspected they each still had feelings for the other, but I also knew both respected the sanctity of the vow Father Kilian had taken, and neither, I was certain, would ever act on the emotions that had been left to simmer for close to forty-five years.

I set the yearbook on the desk and turned off the light. Cody was waiting for me. I'd thought about the love affair between Father Kilian and my aunt a lot since she'd shared her secret with me. I couldn't even begin to imagine how difficult the choice that had faced them as teens must have been. Maggie said that as the eldest son in his family, Michael Kilian's destiny was set before he was even born. It was tradition that dictated he would enter the priesthood, just as the eldest sons in the Kilian family had for generations before him.

I tried to imagine taking a step back and watching helplessly as Cody exited my life if he had inherited such a calling. I'm not sure I would have the courage to be as brave or selfless as Maggie if someday I were to find myself in her shoes.

Theresa Lively lived in a small but nicely kept up house in an old neighborhood just east of the church. When we arrived there I noticed the residence was dark. Cody and I rang the bell, but there was no answer. I hated to leave Sydney out in the rain, so I tried the doorknob to the front door, which opened easily. My plan was to simply set the cat inside and reclose the door, but when I leaned in to release the cat I noticed the interior of the house had been destroyed

"It looks like someone vandalized the place," I commented.

I stepped inside with the cat and turned on the light nearest to the front door, with Cody following me. Drawers and cabinets were hanging open, their contents strewn across the floor. Much of the furniture had been displaced and every book in the floor-to-ceiling bookcase was lying in a pile at the foot of the shelving.

"Theresa," I called.

There was no answer. I had a bad feeling about this.

"We'd better call Finn," Cody said.

He made the call while I walked slowly down the hall. I prayed I wouldn't find Theresa's lifeless body, wishing I'd taken Cody's suggestion to call Finn when we'd first found Sydney locked in the confessional. I wasn't sure how I'd live with myself if I were to discover that the extra thirty minutes it had taken to turn the kids over to their parents and make the trip to Theresa's home could have made all the difference in the outcome of the story.

Sydney trotted along beside me as I opened and closed each door in the dark hallway. The first room was a guest bedroom, followed by a bathroom, an office, and then a hall closet. Every room in the small house had been tossed as the living room had, but so far I hadn't found a body, either dead or alive.

When we got to the room at the end of the hall, Sydney scratched to get inside. I really didn't want to open this last door, but the cat seemed quite insistent, so I slowly turned the knob and stepped into the room. I held my breath as I flipped on the overhead light and looked around the space that Theresa obviously used as a bedroom. The dresser drawers were all open, their contents strewn around the room. The closet likewise had been ransacked, and the cosmetics, which I imagined had once been stored on the vanity, had been tossed randomly onto the bed. I slowly let out my breath when I realized this room was as bodiless as the others. What could someone have been looking for that would cause them to carry out such a thorough search of Theresa's private space?

I stepped farther into the room. Sydney followed me inside and then trotted across the room and began scratching at the wall. I frowned. What was the silly cat up to? As far as I could tell, the spot on the wall where he was scratching was nothing more than empty space. I slowly crossed the room and knelt down next to the cat.

"What is it?"

"Meow." The cat continued to scratch at the wall. Maybe there was a mouse in the wall, or maybe the cat was simply reacting to the chaos, but I didn't think so.

The room was paneled with a whitewashed wood product that I imagined looked nice with the cheery fabric used for the comforter and curtains when the room was in order. I ran my hand over the place where Sydney was scratching, looking for anything at all that might have gotten the cat's attention. At first I didn't feel anything. The wall seemed smooth, the texture seamless. I was about to give up and head back toward the front of the house, but then I noticed that one of the boards was loose. It wasn't so loose as to be obvious, and to be honest I most likely wouldn't have noticed it at all if I hadn't been so intent on figuring out what the cat was after. I slowly pulled the piece of paneling away from the sheetrock behind it to find a small metal box hidden inside the wall. I pulled out the box and tried to open it, but it was locked.

"Finn's on his way." Cody walked into the room from behind me. "He said not to touch anything."

I replaced the wood paneling but kept the box.

"What's that?" Cody asked.

"I'm not sure. Sydney led me to it. I'm betting it's important." I looked around the room, which was a complete shambles. "I think I'm going to take Sydney and wait in the car."

"I'll come with you. There really isn't much we can do until Finn gets here."

"I hope Theresa is okay," I said as I cuddled Sydney to my chest. "This place is such a mess. I hate to think what might have happened to her if the person who did this is also responsible for her missing choir practice."

Chapter 2

As I predicted, Theresa Lively wasn't okay. Finn discovered her lifeless body in the trunk of her car shortly after he finished searching her home. Finn speculated that Theresa might have been killed elsewhere, stuffed into her car, and then driven home. He called in a crime scene unit in the hope of finding evidence inside the vehicle that would lead to the killer.

Because I'd found Sydney in the church Finn theorized that Theresa had been abducted from there. I mentioned my idea that it might have been kids who'd locked the cat in the confessional as a prank, but Finn pointed out that it was raining and had been off and on for a good part of the afternoon, so it was unlikely that either the cat or the kids had been out and about that evening. I had to admit that hadn't occurred to me. I was really off my game. Finn was right: Theresa must have been at the church at some point, although I really couldn't imagine why Sydney would have been with her.

Cody and I were allowed to leave once Finn took our statements. Neither of us had eaten, but we had Sydney with us, which would make stopping off for a bite difficult, so we picked up takeout and headed back to my place. Cody seemed to be unusually quiet as we drove through the rain-soaked streets. I suppose it made sense that he had Theresa's murder on his mind, but my intuition told me there was something more.

"Something on your mind?" I inquired.

Cody turned and looked at me. He smiled, but it appeared to be forced. "I'm just trying to figure out who would have wanted to kill Theresa."

"Is there anything else bothering you?" I prodded.

"No. Not really. Why do you ask?"

"Because you've seemed distracted all week. I wanted to talk to you about it on Monday, but you ended up working late, so we never did get together, and then I had to go to Seattle yesterday. This is the first time we've been alone since the weekend, so it's my first opportunity to ask."

Cody didn't answer right away, which made me nervous. Really nervous. He's normally an open book with his thoughts and feelings. I watched his face as he seemed to struggle with some sort of a decision.

"Cody?"

He pulled off the highway and onto the peninsula road. "There is something on my mind," he admitted. "And I do want to talk to you about it, but I'm trying to make up my mind about something first."

"Oh, God. You're going to break up with me."

"What? Of course I'm not going to break up with you." Cody looked shocked by my suggestion, as if that were the furthest thing from his mind, which made me feel somewhat better.

"Then what is it?"

Cody slowed the car as he turned onto the drive that led to the houses on Maggie's estate. "I love you, and someday I hope to marry you and live out the remainder of my life with you. I promise the thing on my mind has nothing to do with my commitment to you. But it does affect us, so I want to be sure before I bring it up."

I felt the fear I had momentarily squelched come charging back.

Cody pulled up in front of my cabin. I wanted to say more, but Siobhan was heading across the lawn that separated the house she lived in with Maggie from mine.

"Finn called and told me about Theresa," Siobhan said as soon as I opened the passenger side door. "Poor Theresa. Do we know what happened?"

"No, I'm afraid not." I opened the side door to my cabin and let my dog Max out for a quick bathroom break. "Cody and I picked up Chinese. Do you want to come in and have some?"

"Sure, I could eat. Finn and I hadn't gotten around to having dinner before you called and he said he'd be late so not to wait. Maggie has taken off on another one of her secret getaways, so I was just going to have a sandwich."

"Maggie left again?"

"Right after breakfast."

I couldn't deny being concerned about Maggie's odd behavior. I know she's an adult and has a right to come and go as she pleases, but she'd been acting secretive lately and I couldn't help but wonder where she was going that would require her to sneak around like a teenager. I found the entire situation to be unsettling.

Cody tossed a match on the fire while I let Max in, dried him off, and then opened a bottle of wine. We all served ourselves and then settled around the table in my breakfast nook. The waves just outside the window were crashing as the wind increased in velocity.

"We might lose power," Siobhan suggested.

"I have a flashlight and some candles in the cupboard. I'll get them out just in case."

"It might be a good idea. I noticed the lights flickering in the big house before you arrived."

In spite of the storm, I really love the coziness of my little cabin. Although it isn't all that well insulated and tends to be drafty, it provides sturdy and secure shelter from the elements. It had originally been built as a summer cabin, but when I'd expressed my desire to move out of my mother's house Maggie had offered to let me move in.

"Do we have any theories about what might have happened to Theresa?" Siobhan asked.

"Not so far. I really can't imagine who would want to hurt her. She seems so nice, and not the least bit confrontational or controversial. The whole situation is beyond odd. I mean, the fact that Finn found her in the trunk of her car is absurd and no matter how hard I try I really can't come up with a logical explanation as to why poor Sydney was locked in the confessional. The whole thing is just too strange."

"What about the box?" Cody asked. "The cat led you to the box; perhaps the solution to the murder is contained inside it."

"I guess we can try to get it open after we eat. It *is* a metal box and it *is* locked."

"I have bolt cutters up at the main house," Siobhan volunteered.

"I have a tool kit in my trunk," Cody offered. "I'm sure I have something that will work."

"The first thing I probably should do after dinner is go and see to the cats in the sanctuary," I said.

"I'll help you," Siobhan offered. "I was actually heading over to do just that when I saw you pull up."

The Harthaven Cat Sanctuary is really Maggie's baby, but I fill in for her when she's away. The sanctuary was built to shelter the island's feral cat population after a law was passed making it legal to dispose of any cats on your property by any means necessary.

After we finished our meal Siobhan and I bundled up and made a mad dash through the rain toward the large indoor/outdoor structure. When we arrived I entered the first cat room, reserved for moms with kittens, and began the process of providing food and water, as well as clean linens and cat box litter. Each cat room has both an indoor and an enclosed outdoor area, where the cats can lie in the sun, climb trees, and romp to their hearts' content.

I picked up one of the resident kittens and cuddled it. Maggie made sure all the kittens born at the facility were given large doses of human interaction. Once they turned eight weeks of age they were spayed or neutered, given shots, and adopted out to new families. The mama cats who could be rehabilitated were likewise altered and then adopted into forever homes.

"Did Maggie give you any hint as to where she might have gone?" I asked Siobhan.

"No. As usual, she simply told me that she would be gone for a couple of days and asked me to let you know. I promised her that we'd look after the cats and she mentioned that Marley knew she was going to be away and had promised to cover for her at the store."

Marley Donnelly was Maggie's best friend and business partner. Between them, they owned and operated the Bait and Stitch, an eclectic shop that sold both fishing and sewing supplies.

"It's so odd the way she keeps disappearing. I mean, where could she possibly be going that she feels the need to keep her destination a secret?"

"Do you think she's having an affair?" Siobhan wondered.

"I honestly doubt it, but even if she does have a guy, so what? She's a single woman. Even if she's meeting a man she really has nothing to hide."

"Unless the man she's having the affair with isn't single."

Siobhan had a point. If Maggie was involved in a relationship with a married man she would have cause to hide it, but Maggie really didn't seem the sort to become involved in anything illicit. Sure, Maggie tended to speak her mind, and that did land her in hot water at times, but she also had a solid moral code that she tended to live her life by.

"You don't think she's sick?"

"Sick?" Siobhan parroted.

"While an affair with a married man isn't Maggielike at all, trying to prevent us from worrying is *very* Maggielike. What if she's sick with something potentially terminal, like cancer, and she doesn't want to worry us, so she just disappears without a word when it's time for her treatments?"

Siobhan frowned. I could tell she was considering my theory. As much as I hoped it wasn't true, it made more sense than any other theory I'd managed to come up with so far.

"Do you really think she'd lie about something like that?"

"She might," I answered.

"Yeah, I'm afraid I have to agree. Hiding a serious illness sounds exactly like something she might do. How can we find out for sure?"

I paused to think about Siobhan's question. We could ask Marley. Of course even if Maggie confided in her, I sort of doubted Marley would spill her secret. Going through Maggie's stuff seemed like an invasion of privacy, but maybe the next time she announced her departure prior to leaving I could follow her. I mean, it really isn't spying if you just happen to be going in the same direction as someone you just happen to be worried about.

I've talked to Cody about the situation and he thinks I should just butt out. He insists Maggie is an adult and entitled to her secrets. It isn't that I don't think Maggie has a right to live her life as she sees fit without interference from the nieces she has been nothing but wonderful to. But I do worry about her. A lot.

"I'm not sure we can know for sure unless Maggie decides to fill us in on what's going on," I eventually answered.

Siobhan looked at me in the way only a sister who really knows you can. "Is something else wrong? I mean in addition to the fact that Maggie is being secretive and Theresa has been murdered."

"Cody is being secretive as well. I tried to talk to him about it, but he said he needs to make up his mind about something. At first I thought he was planning to break up with me, but he says it isn't that."

"Of course it's not that. Cody loves you. He's planning to build a life with you. If he needs to work out whatever it is he's dealing with, I'd give him some space. I don't know what's on his mind, but I do know he'd never hurt you."

"I guess you're right."

After the sanctuary was cleaned and all the cats fed, Siobhan and I headed back to the cabin. Cody had managed to open the box and the contents were laid out on the table. There was only one item: a small black notebook.

I picked it up and looked inside. Most of the book contained blank pages, but there were a few with numbers and letters across the top, followed by dollar amounts below.

"What do you think this represents?" Siobhan asked.

"Maybe bank accounts?" I speculated. There were five pages in all that followed this pattern.

"If the numbers across the top are bank account numbers they aren't for our local bank," Cody supplied. "Unless they're abbreviations, or perhaps some type of code."

"I'm going to assume the notes in this book are an important clue as to what's going on, but what do we do with them?" I thumbed through the book, trying to make sense of what I was looking at. "If these amounts represent actual dollars we're talking about a lot of money."

Cody looked over my shoulder. "I'd say it's a ledger of some sort, but Theresa didn't seem like someone who'd have a lot of money, and there must be almost a hundred grand written down here. Maybe more. Theresa lived in a nice house in a decent neighborhood, but it was small, and she drove a decent car but certainly not a luxury model."

"Maybe it isn't her money. Or maybe she's keeping track of something else," I suggested.

"Like what?" Siobhan asked.

"I have no idea."

"Maybe we should just turn the book over to Finn," Siobhan said.

I paused before responding. Siobhan had a point. Finn was the actual cop around here, and I had no reason to doubt he'd do everything in his power to find Theresa's killer. Still, there was a small voice in my head that kept nagging at me that we were going to want to refer back to this information at some later date, and Finn might not be able to provide it. It wasn't unheard of for the sheriff to assign a different deputy to an investigation as serious as the murder of a longtime resident.

"I guess we should give the book to Finn, but I'm going to take a picture of each page first." I took out my phone and began snapping a photo of each page. "Just in case we need to reference them at some point."

I loaded the photos I'd just taken into my computer and then filed them in a folder named Sydney, because the book had come to us directly through Theresa's cat. On the surface the file didn't look to be important, but my intuition told me it was going to be very important indeed. It would be a few days before I understood just how important it actually was.

Chapter 3

Thursday, April 21

I woke the next morning to the sound of waves crashing onto the shore outside my window. By the time Finn had shown up the previous evening and filled us in, it had been really late. I'd hoped Cody would stay over, but he said he wanted to get home to check on Mr. Parsons, the elderly man he lived with. I had a million and one things to see to that day but decided the most important one was to take Max for his morning run along the beach. I'd been busy lately and Max hadn't been getting the attention he deserved. Besides, I felt tense and out of sorts, and there was something relaxing about running on the sand as the waves come onto the shore and the thunder of the tide is the only sound that penetrates the rhythm of your own breathing. It was a cool morning, so I'd bundled up in a heavy sweatshirt and long sweatpants before pulling a knitted cap over my head and long ponytail.

It turned out Finn was able to determine that Theresa Lively had been hit over the head with a blunt object in the parking lot of St. Patrick's. While the forensic team was still gathering information, it appeared, based on the blood they'd found both on the automobile and the asphalt, she was hit as she was either entering or exiting her car. She was then dragged around to the rear of the vehicle, where she was dumped into the trunk. The killer had used her keys to drive to her home and park the car in her garage. So far Finn hadn't found any fingerprints other than Theresa's, so it was being assumed that the killer either wore gloves or had been very careful.

The thing I found the most interesting was that Sydney was found in the confessional. If Theresa was just arriving at the church, why was the cat inside and how had he gotten locked in the confessional? If she was leaving rather than arriving, it still didn't explain why the cat was inside. The only thing I could come up with was that the killer had grabbed the cat while he was vandalizing Theresa's home, driven him to the church, locked him in the cubicle, and then left. The question was, why in the world would anyone do such a thing?

I took a deep breath as I jogged along the path that paralleled the beach, feeling the tension leave my body as I focused on nothing other than my own breathing and the sound of the sea. There's a rhythm on Madrona that I've found to be true of island living in general. Maybe it's the fact that there's really nowhere to go, or that in general folks tend to stay put rather than move around, but I've found that island living brings a slower pace. Or at least it used to. It was true that with the changes the island had undergone in recent years, the pace of our lives seemed to have been affected to a certain degree.

Finn had interviewed Sister Mary the previous evening. Other than Father Kilian, who was away at the moment, she was the only one who lived on the church property. Sister Mary lived in a small house across the lawn and garden area from the church. She reported that she hadn't visited the church building that afternoon, but she had noticed several cars belonging to members of the St. Patrick's women's group in the parking lot when she left to do errands at around three o'clock. Cody and I had arrived at around five and the parking lot was empty then, so the group members must have vacated the property at some point between three and five. Sister Mary couldn't be certain that Theresa's car was among those present at three. She hadn't had cause to pay close attention to which members of the women's group were on the property.

The only other person we knew for certain was present on the church grounds on Wednesday afternoon was Clifford Dayton. Clifford was the paid janitor at St. Patrick's. While the women's group sees to things such as cleaning the linens, light dusting, flower arrangements, and puttering around in the garden, Cliff takes care of all the heavy cleaning and maintenance. Finn had tried to reach Cliff the previous evening, but he was out and, as far as I knew, hadn't returned his call yet.

Max and I ran along the beach for several miles and then I cut up to the road and turned onto the main highway so I could circle through the business section of Pelican Bay. As I neared the harbor, I turned down the first row of residences, which paralleled the oceanfront road where most of Pelican Bay's businesses could be found.

I decided to pop in on Tansy to ask her about Sydney. In the past Tansy had sent me magical cats to help me with the murder investigations I seemed to be continually getting involved in. Neither Tansy nor her best friend, Bella, would admit or deny being witches, but both women knew things that couldn't be empirically explained. While both Bella and Tansy seemed to be more in tune with the natural rhythms of the universe than most, it's Tansy who demonstrates a level of intuition that's downright disturbing. If Sydney was sent to me by Tansy, he would be the seventh cat she'd put me in contact with. Five of the previous six had helped me solve murders, and one had come to reunite a father with his son.

"Good morning, Bella," I greeted after the tall woman opened her front door in response to my knock.

"Caitlin, how are you, dear? I was just getting ready to head down to the shop, but do come in."

Bella and Tansy own Herbalities, an interesting shop that sells herbal remedies and offers fortune-telling services.

"I'm pretty sandy, but I'd like to speak to Tansy for a minute if she's around."

Bella bent down and petted Max behind the ears. "She's here. Come on inside and have a cup of tea. A little sand and seawater never hurt anyone. I have a few minutes before I need to leave, so I'll join you for a cup as well."

I followed Bella into the cheerful house with the sunny kitchen. I took a seat at the table while Bella ran upstairs to get Tansy.

At first glance the kitchen was much like any other. There were cast-iron pots hanging from a rack, a bouquet of fresh flowers graced the table, a basket of fresh fruit sat on the tile counter, bunches of dried herbs hung from the ceiling, and healthy green potted plants had been set on several surfaces. Upon closer examination, however, visitors soon realized the plants growing in the enclosed sunporch to the rear of the house were actually herbs, and the knickknacks found around the room were talismans strategically placed for specific purposes.

"Cait." Tansy hugged me when she glided into the kitchen in bare feet. "I had a feeling you'd be by, so I made you some of your favorite muffins."

"Thank you; they look delicious." I smiled at the petite, fair-skinned woman with jet-black hair hanging to her waist.

"I guess you're here about Sydney."

I should have known Tansy would get right to the matter at hand. "I assume you sent him to me?"

Tansy frowned. "Actually, no. The fact that you ran into Sydney in the confessional was strictly chance. I'm certain, however, that he can help you, although my instincts tell me this particular situation has many layers and might benefit from the help of another."

I sat back in my chair. "Another?"

Tansy sat down at the table across from me while Bella made the tea. She stared into space, as if trying to get her bearings. I have to admit that the serious look on the face of the normally light and airy witch was making me a little nervous.

"You will be joined by another. A cat named Lucie. She will come to you before the sun sets. I feel conflicting energies. The cats will not like each other initially, but it is important that they work together. You need to make them see this."

"How am I supposed to convince two cats who don't get along to work together?"

Tansy smiled. "You'll find a way."

Great.

"These muffins are delicious."

Bella set a pot of tea and three cups on the table and sat down before pouring the tea into the cups.

"Thank you," Tansy answered. "They're a special recipe I've developed. I had a feeling you would like them. I'll bag some up for you to take to Siobhan. I'm afraid they won't keep until Maggie returns, but I can make another batch for her next week."

"You know Maggie's away?"

"Of course."

I should have figured. Tansy knew everything.

"I don't suppose you could tell me where she's gone off to? Siobhan and I are worried about her."

Tansy looked directly at me. She paused, as if trying to make up her mind about something. "Maggie isn't ill. There's no cause for concern. She's just trying to make up her mind about something and she needs the space to do so."

I smiled in relief. I was still curious about where Maggie was, but if Tansy said she wasn't ill, chances were she wasn't.

"As long as we're on the subject of people making up their minds about things, you wouldn't happen to know what Cody has on his mind?"

Tansy smiled at me with a twinkle of knowing in her eyes. She glanced at Bella, who nodded before taking a sip of her tea. It was sort of creepy the way the two women seemed to communicate without either of them saying a word.

"Cody's secret is not ours to tell," Tansy replied. "He'll tell you when the time is right."

"I'm trying not to worry, but it's hard. I want to help. He seems distressed, or maybe it's more like confused."

"Cody is facing a difficult decision, but I wouldn't worry. My intuition tells me that everything will work itself out as it should."

I wasn't sure if that made me feel better or not, but I didn't suppose there was anything I could do about the situation at that point in time, so I chatted with Tansy and Bella a while longer and then Max and I headed back toward the peninsula. I fed Max and headed over to the sanctuary to feed the cats before heading in to shower and get ready for work. I love the bookstore my best friend Tara and I run, but today I wished I could just stay home and work on a few of the theories I'd begun to develop.

"Everything is set for the advertising for the sale this weekend," I informed Tara later that morning.

"Great. I know it's only a two-day sale, but I'm really hoping for a good turnout. We could use a boost to our income after a couple of slow months."

"Where are we with the new inventory?"

"Destiny catalogued it into the computer before she left for her lessons, and I have half of it set out. The rest is in the back."

Destiny was our part-time employee.

"Did we get in any more of the new spring mugs? It seems they've been selling faster than we could put them on the shelves."

"I set out the last batch yesterday and by the end of the day they were gone. I guess I'll double the order next time."

"Or triple it. The mugs have been our best-selling item the past couple of months. We should start planning a summer design now."

"I've sketched out a few ideas. I'll show them to you later. The ferry will be here in a few minutes. We should get the coffee bar ready."

Tara started a fresh pot of coffee and then began refilling the other supplies we'd need to make the hot beverages we were known for. So far it seemed that combining a coffee bar with a bookstore and a cat lounge had proven to be a popular and profitable idea. January and February had been our slowest months since opening the store the previous August, but that was probably to be expected. The winter months were the slowest on the island in general.

"By the way," Tara filled the grinder with coffee beans as I gathered the boxes we'd unpacked in preparation for disposal, "Jill Post was in yesterday while you were at lunch. I meant to tell you about her visit when you got back, but it slipped my mind. She asked about a kitten for Tillie. Apparently, Tillie saw a longhaired orange female when her mom was in picking up her order. I told her I'd ask you if she was still available."

"She might be. I have an application I'm checking out from a woman who lives on Orcas Island, but unless my information is incorrect, it looks like she already has nine cats. I'm sure she loves cats and would probably take decent care of the little gal, but ten cats? I left a message for a friend of mine who lives on the island; she's going to pop by her place to do a quickie home visit. If she does indeed have nine cats, I think I'll decline the application. I'll call Jill either way."

"Yesterday was so hectic I never did ask you about your trip to Seattle on Tuesday. How'd it go?"

"Great. I think I accomplished everything I set out to do. I do need to follow up on a couple of the donors I spoke to about the cat sanctuary. Everyone seemed willing to help support the project, but there were a few who needed to speak to other people."

"It's a good cause most folks will want to get behind."

"It is. Oh, you'll never guess who I ran into on the ferry on the way home— Felicity Danielson," I said, without waiting for Tara to try.

"I haven't seen her in at least a couple of years."

Felicity had gone to high school with Siobhan. Although she'd grown up on the island, she'd gotten a job in Seattle a couple of years ago and hadn't returned since.

"She said this was the first time she's been back since she left. I mentioned she might have waited for a nicer time of year to visit with all the rain we've been having, but she said she had some business to take care of that couldn't wait. She looked worried and sort of tense. I hope everything's okay."

"I just spoke to her mother last week and she didn't mention any problems. Of course she also didn't mention Felicity was coming home."

"I kind of think it was a last-minute thing. It sounded like she hadn't really been planning to come home, and I got the feeling she hadn't talked to her mom lately."

"I wonder if she had a falling out with her mom. That would explain why she moved from the island so suddenly and never once came back to visit."

"I guess. Did the new shipment of books we ordered ever come in?"

"Yeah, they arrived yesterday as well. I figured we'll unpack them after the midday crowd thins out a bit."

By the time we got the supplies ready the ferry had debarked and the store became crowded. Tara and I worked in perfect synchronicity as we served drinks, rang up purchases, and chatted with tourists, friends, and neighbors. Given the fact that our primary source of revenue came from travelers coming to and from the ferry, our customers tended to come in waves.

I smiled at Felicity as she entered the store and made her way to the counter.

"We were just talking about you," Tara said as she came around the counter and gave her a hug. "I'm so glad you finally came home for a visit."

"It's been hard to get away. It's hard to believe it's been more than two years. And

I can't believe how much has changed. I heard Destiny Paulson had a baby."

"A little boy, just before Christmas," Tara confirmed.

"It's so strange to think of Destiny with a baby. I used to babysit her and her sisters. It seems like yesterday she was running around in that little pink ballerina dress she used to love so much."

"I remember that dress." I laughed. "She wore it to church every Sunday for months."

"Is she doing okay? I heard the dad isn't in the picture."

"She is," Tara confirmed. "She's living with me and working at the bookstore while she finishes high school through a homeschool program. She has plans to go to college in the fall. I think she's going to do just fine with single motherhood."

"I'm glad to hear that. I always did like Destiny."

"So what can I get you to drink?" Tara asked.

"A latte would be great."

I noticed Felicity's smile didn't quite reach her eyes.

"Did you get your business taken care of?" I asked.

She nodded. "Do you think we could talk?" Felicity looked around the room. "Somewhere private?"

The crowd had mostly thinned, so it appeared Tara could handle the rest on her own. "Sure. Let's go into the cat lounge. There's no one in there right now except for the cats."

Felicity accepted her beverage from Tara and then followed me into the glassed-in room. As soon as we got there she began to pace nervously.

"What can I do for you?" I sat down on one of the sofas and two of the cats jumped into my lap. I'd been on my feet for hours; it felt good to take a break.

"I take it you haven't checked your e-mail recently?"

"No. Not since first thing this morning. Why?"

"I think I might be in trouble." Felicity sat down next to me.

I frowned. "What kind of trouble?"

"When you check your e-mail you'll find that you've received a video that was sent to me and copied to you."

"A video? I'm confused. What video?"

"One of me arguing with Theresa Lively shortly before she was murdered."

"You didn't do it, did you?"

"No." Felicia took a deep breath. She looked around the room, as if trying to gather her thoughts. She looked more nervous than I'd ever seen her. "Of course not, but we did argue, and when I saw the video I realized it was going to make me look guilty."

"Why don't you start at the beginning?" I suggested.

"Theresa was blackmailing me. She had been for more than two years. I decided I'd finally had enough, so I came to the island to confront her."

"Blackmailing you? For what?"

"I really can't say, but the why isn't as important as the fact that she was, and I figure I'm going to be blamed for a murder I didn't commit."

"Okay, tell me about the video."

"After I checked into the hotel I called Theresa and told her we needed to talk. She said she would, but rather than meeting at her home she wanted to see me at the church the following afternoon. I agreed to meet her there. We argued, I threatened her, and then I left. She was very much alive at the time, I swear. When Mom told me this morning that Theresa had been murdered I freaked out, but I didn't start to panic until I checked my e-mail. Someone sent me a video of my conversation with Theresa, and I noticed they sent a copy to you too."

I decided to take a moment to try to process everything Felicia had told me. Theresa didn't seem at all the type to be a blackmailer, but I guess you never really knew what went on behind the closed doors of another person's life.

"How much did you pay Theresa?"

"Five hundred dollars a month for the past twenty-eight months."

I thought back to the notebook. One of the pages did have a list of five-hundred-dollar payments. I'd have to check my file when I got home, but I was willing to bet there were twenty-eight of them. "How exactly did you pay Theresa?"

"She has a dummy website. It appears as if she's selling jewelry. Every month she sends me a link and I log on to the site and buy something for five hundred dollars."

"Do you have the address for this website?"

"No. I don't know how to access the site other than using the link."

"Do you have the link with you?"

"I have last month's link on my laptop, but I doubt it will work. There's a new link every month."

I jotted down my e-mail address. "Can you forward any links you still have to me?"

"I can, but what am I going to do about the video?"

I paused to consider the situation. There was really only one possible answer. "The person who sent the video may send it to others as well. I recommend you tell Finn what you just told me. Maybe he'll believe you if you go to him before he finds out about the blackmail some other way."

"I was afraid you were going to say that." Felicity got up from the sofa. "I'll forward the last link as soon as I get back to my hotel room. Thanks for listening."

"Did you happen to go over to Theresa's house after you argued? Perhaps to look for whatever evidence she had on you?"

"No. I went back to the hotel and tried to watch a movie. Why do you ask?"

"Because someone trashed Theresa's place. It looked as if whoever did it was looking for something."

"Do you think they found what they were looking for?"

"I have no idea."

Felicity paled. "What if they found the evidence Theresa used to blackmail me?"

"If the person who vandalized Theresa's house was looking for this sort of evidence and found it, I suppose you may have another problem altogether."

Felicity closed her eyes and tilted her head toward the ceiling.

"I don't know what Theresa had on you, but maybe you should just come clean. If you do, the thing that's been hanging over your head all this time will no longer have the power to hurt you."

"It's bad. Really bad. The sort of thing you confess to your maker but no one else."

I couldn't imagine what Felicity had done, but she looked terrified.

I returned to the bookstore side of Coffee Cat Books after Felicity left. It occurred to me that if she was being blackmailed and the payments she made to Theresa were being recorded in the small black notebook I'd found, the other pages might represent payments made by other victims. If Theresa was blackmailing other people on the island, there was a very good chance one of her other victims also had decided to stop the money drain.

"What was that all about?" Tara asked after the last customer left.

"Felicity wanted my help." I shared the gist of my conversation with Tara.

"Blackmailing? For what?"

"Felicity didn't say, but if she was willing to fork over fourteen grand to keep it quiet her secret must be a doozy."

"I'll say. Now I'm curious."

I grabbed a bottle of water from the refrigerator and twisted off the cap. "Me too. I can't imagine what sort of information Theresa must have had that would be worth all that money, but what I do know is that, in spite of Felicity's assurance that she didn't kill Theresa, I can't help but consider her a suspect."

"She certainly does have a motive," Tara agreed.

I went to the Coffee Cat Books' computer and logged into my e-mail. I found the video that showed Theresa standing on the altar of the church arguing with Felicity. Felicity was correct; their argument did look damaging. She could clearly be heard threatening to kill Theresa if she leaked the information she had on her. Whoever had filmed the argument had stopped recording before either party left, so there was no way to know definitively what had happened next.

"Wow; she really does look guilty," Tara commented.

"Yeah, she does. Finn will have little choice but to arrest her if he sees this.

She said she was being blackmailed and I have a feeling there may be others. I need to run home to pick up my laptop. I found a notebook in Theresa's bedroom last night and I think it might have been the log where she kept a record of her blackmail income. I gave Finn the pad, but I kept photos of all the pages that had writing on them. If what Felicity told me matches up with one of the pages, I think we can assume the others represent the income from other blackmail victims. It seems important to work on figuring out the rest of the notes. Will you be okay alone for a bit?"

"Yeah. It's slow, and now that the rain is back I don't anticipate foot traffic will pick up. Take as much time as you need."

"Great. I shouldn't be long."

Chapter 4

When I pulled up in front of my cabin the first thing I noticed was a white cat sitting on my porch swing. "Lucie, I assume," I greeted the cat, figuring it was the second feline sleuthing partner Tansy had mentioned to me. I twisted the knob, opened the door, and let us both inside. Max trotted over to greet me while Sydney hissed at the new arrival.

Lucie hunched her back and growled in return.

"Look, I don't have time for kitty theatrics. Tansy mentioned you wouldn't get along, but I don't have time for a cat fight. I'll be back later this afternoon, and in the meantime I need the two of you to try to get along."

Neither cat answered, not that I expected them to, but at least they stopped hissing at each other. I let Max out for a few minutes while I logged onto my computer. I quickly opened it to the file with the five-hundred-dollar deposits and verified that there were indeed twenty-eight of them, dating back twenty-eight months. The payments must have started just before Felicity moved to Seattle.

Across the top of the page was a header with letters and numbers: FDB239-362419.

The FD must stand for Felicity Danielson. This was useful information; now I could assume the first two letters in each code were the blackmail victim's initials, which narrowed things down a bit. Of course I didn't actually know that the other pages represented other victims. It was entirely possible I was barking up the wrong tree.

I watched as Lucie jumped up onto the counter to hiss at Sydney, who looked ready to pounce from his perch on the back of the sofa. I wondered if it was safe to leave them alone in the cabin with no one other than Max around to referee. I could take one of them over to the cat sanctuary, but Tansy did say they needed to work together, so perhaps it would be better to let them get used to each other.

"What exactly is the problem?" I asked aloud.

Lucie jumped from the counter onto the bookshelf, knocking a photo of me standing in front of my first car onto the floor. Normally I would pay attention to such a sign, but I couldn't imagine what a photo of me standing on the side of the highway near the cliff at Shell Beach would have to do with anything.

I picked Lucie up and took her up to the bedroom. I wanted the cats to get along, but I didn't want them to destroy the cabin in my absence, so I decided it was best to separate them for the time being. I already had a cat box and food and water dish set up for Sydney downstairs, so I set Lucie up with her own conveniences upstairs and made sure all the windows were firmly closed. I then begged Lucie not to destroy my bedroom and closed the door behind me. When I returned home that evening I'd get the cats together for a little kitty couples counseling.

Max came back from his romp and I gave him fresh water, then packed up my laptop and headed back to the bookstore. Maybe Tara could help me make sense of the rest of the code written across the top of the pages in the notebook. If not during business hours, perhaps I'd have her and Cody over that evening after the planning meeting for a good old-fashioned brainstorming session. It had been a while since we'd had to assemble the gang to create a murder board. I was pretty sure

Siobhan would want to join us as well, if she wasn't busy with Finn.

"Maybe the HS represents another person involved in the same blackmail," Tara suggested later that afternoon, after the store had cleared out and we had a break. "Or maybe the subject of the blackmail. How does it compare to the other pages?"

I made a list of the headers for each of the five pages, which I then put on the counter in front of us.

FDB239-362419
VWSP126
CMCC312
MHMB241-0668
TOSB

"There really doesn't seem to be a pattern other than that there are letters followed in most cases by numbers, but the last one doesn't even have any numbers," Tara observed. "It's going to be hard to figure out without a frame of reference."

"Yeah, even if the first two letters are initials I don't see how we can narrow it down without further information."

"CM could be Cicely Michaels," Tara speculated.

"Yeah, but TO could be Tara O'Brian," I pointed out.

"True. We really have nothing. What are we going to do?"

I paused to consider Tara's question. To be honest, I had no idea how to proceed. If we could figure out the first one, I thought maybe we could see a pattern of some sort. "Do you want to come over and brainstorm after the meeting at the church?"

"Will Danny be there?"

"No. He hasn't been around a whole lot lately."

Danny is my second oldest brother. He and Tara used to date. Sort of. Anyway, they'd realized it wasn't working out, so they'd split. Danny had moved on the next day, but Tara was having a harder time of it. She seemed fine most of the time, but I didn't think she was ready to spend much time with him in an intimate situation such as the sort that can be created when a group of people work toward a common goal.

"Okay," Tara agreed. "I'm in."

"I'm going to ask Cody as well. If Finn and Siobhan aren't busy I'm going to ask her. I would ask Finn, but I'm afraid he'll be less than happy that I took photos of the pages in the notebook before I gave it to him."

Tara and I continued to discuss the various possibilities a while longer but were really getting nowhere. We were about to call it a day when Destiny walked in.

"Hey, guys. Whatcha doin'?"

"Trying to figure out a puzzle," I answered.

"I'm good at puzzles. Can I help?"

I explained about the notebook I'd found in Theresa's house and the codes it contained. I also filled her in on the fact that Felicity Danielson had confessed to the fact that she was being blackmailed and we were pretty sure the FD in FDB239-362419 referred to her.

"We have no idea what the rest of it means," Tara added.

"You said she was being blackmailed. What if the rest, or at least part of the rest, refers to a place?"

"A place?" I asked.

"I might be way off, but B239 reminds me of a locker location. When I went to the high school my locker number was B260 because my locker was located in the B building."

"Why would Theresa have a locker at the high school?" Tara asked. "She hasn't gone to high school for quite some time. Neither has Felicity."

"My locker was just down from the music room. B239 would probably be about as close as you could get to the music room door. Mrs. Lively helped out with the music program at the school. Maybe she was assigned a locker to keep her music and stuff in."

I glanced at Tara. "Destiny's theory makes sense."

"It's slow today. I guess you could go check it out. We'll need to convince the school administration to let us into the locker."

"I can go," Destiny offered. "I'm on campus all the time anyway to use the science lab."

"You'll need the combination," I pointed out.

Destiny looked at the code once again. "My combination was 32-46-13. How much do you want to bet that 26-24-19 will open locker B239?"

I shrugged. "It's worth a try."

I drove Destiny to the high school but waited in the car while she went inside. Although she was being homeschooled by Sister Mary so she could have both a flexible schedule, so she could work and take care of her son, and could graduate a year early, she still did her science work in the school lab. While my being on campus might draw attention, her being there was a regular occurrence.

Ten minutes after she went into the building she emerged again.

"So?" I asked.

"The combination opened the locker, which was filled with sheet music. I did find this taped to the top of the locker, though." Destiny held up a thumb drive.

"Maybe that holds the evidence Theresa was using to blackmail Felicity," I suggested.

"There's only one way to find out."

We returned to the bookstore and I logged on to my laptop and inserted the thumb drive. There was only an audio file on it. My mouth dropped open as I listened to Felicity's voice.

It was an accident. We didn't mean to hurt anyone. We were just messing around after a party. It seemed like he came out of nowhere. One minute we were singing to the radio and the next we saw this car coming right at us.

Felicity stopped talking, but I could tell she was crying. It felt like maybe someone was responding to her words, but we couldn't hear what was being said.

Eventually Felicity began speaking again. *I know we should have stopped, but we panicked when we realized we'd swerved into the other lane and caused the accident. We totally freaked and drove away. The next morning when I heard the old guy had drowned I was devastated, but it was too late to do things differently.*

Again Felicity stopped talking, as if she were listening to someone. She was sobbing loudly by this point. I listened carefully to see if I could make out a second voice, but all I heard was static.

I can't tell you. It won't do any good. My telling won't bring the old guy back. Besides, I promised I wouldn't tell, and you can't either. Right?

The tape ended.

"Wow," Tara said. "What do you think that was all about and who do you think she was talking to?"

"Maybe Theresa?" Destiny speculated. "That could be how she knew."

"I don't think so," I said. It seemed odd that we could only hear Felicity's voice and not the voice of the person she was speaking to.

"What accident do you think she's talking about?" Tara asked.

I thought about it. The payments had begun twenty-eight months ago. The accident had to have occurred prior to that. I picked up my phone and called Cody. The prior owner of the newspaper hadn't digitized anything, and while Cody was working on the upgrade, there was still a lot of information to upload. I asked Cody to look at the news articles that were written between twenty-eight and thirty-two months ago. I was willing to bet the conversation we'd heard had taken place shortly after the accident.

"A sixty-eight-year-old man named Homer Woodford drowned after his car was run off the road near Shell Beach," Cody informed me. "He was alone in the car and they never found out what it was that caused him to veer from his lane and go over the cliff."

"I think I know," I answered. "Can you come over tonight?"

"I was planning to. I'll bring pizza."

I hung up and looked at Tara and Destiny. "It seems Felicity and whoever the other half of the *we* she was referring to were responsible for the death of a motorist who drowned off Shell Beach."

"I remember that," Tara contributed. "They never did find out what happened."

"I guess we know. We should call Finn. I hate to turn Felicity in, but she was responsible for a man's death."

"Yeah," Tara agreed. "It's the right thing to do."

Later that evening I sat with Cody, Tara, Finn, and Siobhan as we ate pizza and discussed Theresa's murder. When Finn had gone to the hotel Felicity had said she was staying in, he found out she had already checked out. Personnel confirmed she was on the last ferry of the day to the mainland. We assumed she was heading home, so Finn called Seattle PD to follow up.

"So who do you think she was talking to?" Siobhan asked. "The tape sounds odd. Like she was talking to someone in a soundproof room. And the fact that we can't hear the response of the other person is sort of creepy."

"The tape could have been edited if Theresa didn't want anyone to know who the other person was," Tara suggested.

"Of course that would assume Theresa would think someone other than herself might listen to it," Cody pointed out.

"The thing that's strangest is that Felicity said she never told anyone what happened and had no idea how Theresa knew what she found out," I added. "I'm not sure why she would say that if it wasn't true."

"Well, she obviously told someone," Siobhan commented.

"Her maker," I shouted. "Felicity said she'd never told anyone other than her maker."

"She was talking to God?" Tara asked.

"Indirectly," I theorized. "She said something about confessing to her maker."

"The confessional," Siobhan caught on. "Theresa bugged the confessional."

Oh, God. I quickly thought back to the juicy tidbits I'd confessed over the years. I supposed there was nothing too scandalous.

"How did Theresa manage to bug the confessional?" Finn asked.

"She's at the church all the time," I told him. "She not only played the organ and piano for both the children's and adult choirs but she was part of the women's group that helps out with light cleaning and maintenance."

"So she's been listening in on the confessions of her neighbors and using the juiciest ones to blackmail people," Cody summarized.

"It would seem. And it would seem that one of the people she was milking had had enough and killed her," I said. "Locking the cat in the confessional must have been symbolic."

"Question is, which of Theresa's victims killed her?" Tara asked.

"Maybe Felicity did," Siobhan theorized. "You said she spoke to Theresa and they argued. You told her to come clean with Finn but instead she fled. Only guilty people flee."

Siobhan had a point, but my gut told me that Felicity wasn't the one who'd killed Theresa. There was no doubt about it: If we were going to figure out what happened, we'd need to put our heads together to break the rest of the codes.

Chapter 5

Friday, April 22

I woke the next morning with a new lease on life. Not only were Sydney and Lucie both sitting in the bedroom window looking out at the seagulls that were diving for their breakfast but the weather service had reported a significant rise in temperature beginning today, and the brilliant sunshine streaming through my window seemed to support that very prediction.

"It seems the two of you are getting along better."

Neither cat turned to look at me, but they weren't fighting or hissing at each other in spite of the fact that they sat only inches apart. I slid out of bed, pulled a warm sweatshirt over my head and knee-high slippers onto me feet, then headed down to make the coffee. Once the coffee brewed I poured some into my favorite pink Coffee Cat Books mug, added a splash of milk, and headed out onto the deck with Max trailing along behind me.

The sun on my shoulders and the clear blue sky lent legitimacy to the fact that the long and lazy days of summer I'd been longing for all winter were indeed just beyond the horizon. I sat down in my favorite chair and curled my legs up under my body. I took a long sip of my hot beverage as I let the sound of the seagulls in flight and the waves gently lapping onto the shore calm my spirit and warm my soul.

The gang and I had stayed up until the wee hours trying to decipher the remaining four codes with absolutely no luck. Finn took the link Felicity had forwarded for the fake jewelry site to which she'd claimed to have made her payments to Theresa and promised to track down the source of the money trail. We hoped the other victims had made payments to the same site; if we could identify the source of the payments, maybe we could discover who the other four suspects were.

I was about to get up and head inside to make some breakfast when Mr. Parsons's dog, Rambler, came running up to greet Max, who was playing in the waves in front of my cabin. I looked down the beach to see Cody walking toward me. Normally, an early morning visit from Cody would bring feelings of gladness, but today I had the sense he had something serious on his mind.

"Just in time for my special egg and potato hash," I greeted lightly in spite of the knot in my stomach.

"I'm not really hungry, but you go ahead."

"Something on your mind?"

Cody sat down in the chair next to me. He looked out toward the horizon. I tried to read his face, but there were so many emotions present I couldn't even begin to guess where this conversation might be going.

"Do you want to talk?" I tried again.

Cody turned to look at me. "Actually, I do. Are you warm enough. Do you want to go inside?"

"I'm fine." My heart was pounding in my chest. "What's up?"

Cody took my hand in his. He wound his fingers through mine and gave my hand a squeeze. I could see the hesitation on his face, but I decided to wait patiently for him to speak. The longer he hesitated the larger the knot in my stomach grew. There was no way this conversation wasn't going to be painful. I braced for the worst.

"I need to go out of town for a few days."

I waited for him to continue. I wasn't sure what to say at this point.

"I'll be leaving on the noon ferry and I should be back Monday afternoon."

I took a deep breath. "Okay. Can you tell me where you're going?"

"Kitsap."

I knew there was a naval base located on the Kitsap Peninsula, across Puget Sound from Seattle. It wasn't all that far away, and a trip there shouldn't be causing Cody this much angst unless … Cody had been in the Navy prior to moving back to Madrona Island, but as far as I knew he had officially left the service and was 100 percent a civilian now. Surely he wasn't going to re-up.

"Kitsap? Why?"

Cody took a deep breath before he continued. Oh, God, he *was* going to re-up.

"Before I left the Navy I submitted a report to my superiors that detailed a new training method for the SEAL program. I felt then, as I do now, that the suggestions I came up with would improve the training the men and women received and, in the long run, save lives. I guess the Navy has finally gotten around to looking at my report and they agree. They want me to meet with a small committee to discuss the changes. If after they hear what I have to say they still believe the changes will improve the quality of the education the SEAL candidates receive, they'll work out a plan to incorporate my suggestions."

"That's wonderful." I hugged Cody. I was so relieved. This was what was causing him all this angst?

Cody hugged me back. He seemed to be holding on tighter than was necessary, but after his withdrawal during the past several weeks I didn't mind.

"There's more," Cody said after he released me.

"More?"

"The committee is meeting at Kitsap to make my meeting them this weekend convenient for me. If the changes I've suggested are approved they want me to work with the committee to create the new curriculum."

"Okay, I guess that makes sense. Will you have to spend a lot of time at Kitsap?"

"Not at all. I will, however, need to spend six months to a year in Tampa."

"Florida?"

Cody didn't answer, but I could tell by the look on his face that yes, he was referring to Florida.

"But what about the newspaper? And Mr. Parsons? And us?"

Cody tilted his head down and ran his hands through his hair. "Trust me, I've thought of nothing else since they approached me. I'm finally starting to turn a profit after months of hard work modernizing the *Madrona Island News*. There's no way I want that all to be for nothing. And Mr. Parsons seems to really need me. I know he lived alone before I came back to the island, but he's never seemed to bounce back to his old self after his fall. He's getting old. His body doesn't have the same ability to heal as it used to." Cody looked directly into my eyes. "And you, and the *us* I want us to be, are the most important thing in my life. I can't imagine my life without you. I want to marry you. I want us to raise a family. I want to grow old with you."

"But...?"

"But my ideas are good ones. I honestly believe they'll save lives. I don't know how I can turn my back on the men and women who serve our country each and every day."

"And they can't make the changes without you?"

Cody closed his eyes. He put his hands over his face. He looked so very, very tired. "I don't know. I guess they could, but my sense is they won't. Without me there to spearhead the project my sense is that it will die."

I fought the tears I willed myself not to shed as I looked out toward the horizon. "Are you going to reenlist?"

"No. I would be working with the committee as a civilian. I don't have all the details yet, but I've decided to go to the meeting this weekend to hear what they have to say. I promise I'll come back to talk to you about it before I commit to Tampa, if it comes down to that."

"I appreciate that."

Cody leaned over and kissed me. A long, deep kiss that touched my soul and assured my heart that no matter what, our love would find a way. I kissed him back with everything my heart had to offer. He slowly pulled away, tucked my hair behind my ear, and headed slowly back down the beach.

After Cody faded into the distance I had myself a good cry; then I picked myself up, washed my face, made a hearty breakfast, and reminded myself that I was a mature and independent woman who could do the right thing for her man while presenting a strong and supportive front. Okay, we all know that inside I was a total mess. Just the thought of not seeing Cody for a year made me want to start weeping all over again, but how I felt and how I acted didn't necessarily have to be the same thing.

And a year wasn't forever, I reminded myself. And it might not even be a year. Cody had said six months to a year. And I could visit. I think. I hadn't actually asked that, but it wasn't like he was going overseas. Sure, he'd be about as far from Madrona Island as one could get and still be in the continental United States, but Florida was accessible and I had always wanted to visit the state.

I told myself it would all be fine, and for a brief moment I made myself believe it. Military spouses had to say good-bye to their husbands and wives all the time. If they could do it, I could too. And I would. My heart soared with determination as I got ready for work.

On the way into town I sang aloud every patriotic song I could think of. Or at least the parts I could remember. I visualized myself being strong and fearless as I kissed Cody good-bye while "The Star-Spangled Banner" played in the background and fireworks exploded in the distance.

There was no doubt about it: Caitlin Hart was proud to be an American, and she'd do her part to ensure the safety of our men and women in uniform.

Of course my grit and determination didn't last long once I arrived at the bookstore and filled Tara in.

"Wow," Tara sympathized.

"I know."

"A year. That's so long."

"I know." The first of many newly formed tears streamed down my face.

"And Florida. That's so far."

"I know."

"What are you going to do?"

"I …. don't…know," I forced out between bursts of uncontrollable weeping.

Tara hugged me tightly to her chest while I cried out the last of the tears that my poor dehydrated body could muster.

"It'll be okay," she assured me.

"I know."

"And Cody would be doing a good thing."

"A really good thing." I took a deep, calming breath as I wiped away my tears with the tissue Tara had handed me.

"And we need to make this as easy for him as possible."

"We do." I began to find some of my old determination.

"We can help out at the paper and fill in for him with Mr. Parsons."

"We can and we will."

"So are you okay?" Tara asked.

"Not even a tiny bit. But I'll be fine. I just need time to adapt to the idea that Cody will be gone from my life for a period of time. I won't like it, but it won't kill me."

"That's the spirit."

I think I smiled. It was really hard to know. My face felt sort of numb by this point. I wanted to be brave. I really did. But I have to admit that brave was the last thing I was feeling at that moment in time. What I needed, I decided, was a distraction. Luckily, the first ferry of the day arrived, providing just that.

The half hour before the arrival of the ferry and the hour after it docked were the busiest times of our day. During the summer, when the ferry service was frequent, there was rarely a break in the action, but during the winter and early spring months the ferry only docked three times, creating a customer flow of too many to handle followed by hours of absolutely no customers at all.

"Tall nonfat latte to go," Carissa Morton, an island local and volunteer coach for the girl's high school softball team, ordered.

"Coming right up. By the way, how did your game go on Wednesday? I wasn't able to make it."

"We won. Five to three," Carissa confirmed. "That should put us in first place."

"Congratulations. I'm sorry I missed it, but I had choir that night."

"It's hard to take the time when you're trying to run a business and do volunteer work. I'm lucky the law office where I work allows me to work a flexible schedule."

I knew Carissa worked for Brown and Bidwell, the largest law firm on Madrona Island. Brown and Bidwell had a good reputation and was able to attract business from the neighboring islands as well, making it one of the largest law offices in the county.

"Tara mentioned you got a raise and bought yourself a new car."

"I did. And the raise came just in the nick of time. I'd been keeping the old one together with chewing gum and baling wire, but I think my luck had about run out."

"I know what you mean. My old clunker is on its last legs as well, but with the new business it's hard to justify monthly payments. Maybe if we have a good summer."

"If you make it through the off season you should be fine. The summer crowd should begin arriving in a few weeks."

I poured steamed milk into the to-go cup. "I guess you heard about Theresa Lively."

Carissa nodded. "It's such a shame."

I couldn't help but notice the huge grin on Carissa's face, which seemed to convey glee rather than something more appropriate, like sadness or regret.

"Did you know Theresa well?" I asked as I rang up the purchase.

"Not really." Carissa handed me a five-dollar bill. "We did some business together, but other than that we didn't really travel in the same circles."

I handed Carissa her change. She thanked me and turned to leave, and I watched her go with a spring in her step.

As soon as the last customer left, I pulled out the list I had made of the codes in Theresa's pad. There was one that began with CM. Could CM stand for Carissa Morton? Her response to Theresa's death seemed suspect at best. I shared my theory with Tara, who agreed that

Carissa seemed just a bit too happy about the murder of one of her neighbors.

"If Carissa was one of Theresa's victims there must be evidence that can prove our theory, but where?" I asked Tara as she reconciled the cash register before we locked up for the day.

"The code is CMCC312," Tara mused. "If the CM really does stand for Carissa Morton the CC must refer to the location of the evidence. Or at least it must if it follows the same pattern as the code she used to keep track of Felicity's payments."

"Okay, so what could CC mean?"

Tara thought about it. "Theresa used a locker to hide the evidence she had on Felicity. Maybe all the hiding places are lockers. Where else are there lockers on Madrona Island other than the high school?"

"That new gym that opened up in Harthaven does. I honestly don't see Theresa as having a gym membership, however, and I'm pretty sure you have to be a member to have a locker there. Besides, the gym is called Bodies in Motion; I don't see how you could get CC out of that."

"What about the community center?" Tara suggested. "They have lockers, and

CC could definitely stand for community center."

"I bet you're right. That would be perfect. If it is a locker at the community center, the 312 must be the locker number."

"Yeah, but there's no combination given."

"Don't need one. I had a locker when I taught that fitness class, and each owner brings their own combination lock. I still have the bolt cutters we used to cut off the lock on the box I found in Theresa's wall. We'll just cut the lock off locker 312 and hope it's what we're looking for."

The store was closed, so Tara agreed to go with me. There was a Jazzercise class going on in the main room of the center and there were a lot of people about, but luckily, the shower room, where the lockers were, was empty. I used the bolt cutters to liberate the lock, and then, after quickly glancing at the envelope filled with financial documents I found inside to make sure they pertained to Carissa, I slipped it under my jacket and Tara and I headed to my cabin.

Chapter 6

"I guess we should call Finn," Tara said an hour later.

I'm not exactly a wiz when it comes to accounting, but Tara knew what she was looking at, and according to her, it looked as if Carissa had been embezzling from her employer. It took someone pretty gutsy to steal money from a law firm.

"Yeah, I guess we'd better. Although..."

"Although what?" Tara asked.

"What if Carissa isn't our killer? If it's made public that Carissa has been embezzling money and a link is made between her crime and Theresa's death, whichever of the other three blackmail victims who did kill Theresa will have a heads-up that we're on to things."

"True, but if Carissa is stealing money she should be brought to justice, and we don't really know that Carissa didn't kill Theresa."

"Actually, we do. There was a softball game on Wednesday on Orcas Island. There's no way Carissa could have killed Theresa if Finn is correct in his assertion that she'd already been dead for several hours before her body was found. The ferry from Orcas wouldn't have returned with the team until after five, and Finn thinks Theresa was killed between three and five."

"I still think we need to call him. Whether or not to arrest Theresa should be his decision," Tara insisted.

"Yeah, you're right. I'll do it now. Maybe I'll see if he and Siobhan want to join us for dinner. I'm starving."

"Me too. I'll check your cupboards to see what we can whip up."

It turned out that once Finn confirmed Carissa was off the island when Theresa was killed, he agreed we should sit on the information concerning the embezzlement for a few days, but only for a few days. We needed to identify the other three victims of Theresa's blackmail scheme and we needed to do it quickly, before Carissa or anyone else was on to us.

I stared at my computer screen, which displayed the final three codes.

VWSP126

MHMB241-0668

TOSB

"I'm afraid nothing is jumping out at me," I commented just as Finn's phone rang.

He looked at the caller ID, then answered, "Finnegan here."

I waited as he listened to the person on the other end of the line.

"Okay. I'll be right there." Finn turned and looked at Siobhan. "One of the residents who lives near the high school reported a break-in. I need to check it out. I'll call you tomorrow."

"Okay, but be careful," Siobhan responded as Finn gave her a quick peck on the lips before leaving through the side door.

"This is the second break-in at the high school this month," Siobhan informed us after Finn had left. "I feel like there's been a shift in the social climate on the island. We've had a lot of families who have lived here for generations move away, only to be replaced by rich folks from the mainland who show up with their spoiled, bored kids."

"Finn thinks it's the rich kids who are vandalizing the school?" I asked.

"He knows so. He caught a couple of the little vandals the last time. They all have parents who can afford to hire attorneys to get them off with nothing more than a slap on the wrist, which doesn't seem to serve as any deterrent to them; they just turn around and do it again. I think I'm going to bring it up at the next island council meeting. It seems like we're going to need to hold the parents responsible for the actions of their teens if we want the vandalism to stop."

"Wow, look at you being all political." I smiled at my sister.

"I *am* the mayor."

"And a darn good one." I returned my attention to the computer screen. "Do you think MH could be Martha Hanford?"

"What would sweet old Martha Hanford have done that Theresa could blackmail her for?" Tara asked.

Tara was right. Martha was a nice old lady who had lived on the island and gone to St. Patrick's Catholic Church the entire eighty-four years she'd been alive. I couldn't see her committing even a teeny tiny sin that would require confession.

"How about Mitch Henrey?" Siobhan suggested. "That guy is pretty creepy. I could see him doing something blackmail-worthy."

"Yeah, but Mitch doesn't go to St. Patrick's," I countered. "In fact, as far as I know, he doesn't go to any church, and he doesn't seem the type to travel in Theresa's circle. Even if he's up to no good it's doubtful Theresa would have found out about it."

"I guess you have a point. If Theresa was bugging the confessional, chances are all her victims go to St. Pat's."

"That's most likely the case, but there are a lot of people who attend St. Pat's with the same initials as our suspects, so guessing really isn't going to get us anywhere."

I was about to log off my computer when Sydney jumped up onto the counter where I was working. He lay down across the keyboard, which prevented me from doing much of anything.

"Did you want something?"

Sydney rolled over onto his back for a quick belly rub before he jumped off the counter and headed for the stairs. He turned around when he got to the bottom, as if he were waiting for me.

"I think he wants you to follow him," Tara said.

"I figured."

"It's kind of creepy the way the cats communicate with you," Siobhan added.

"Creepy but effective so far."

Siobhan, Tara, and I all followed Sydney up the stairs. He ran over to my closet door and began to scratch it. I opened the door and he trotted inside, then jumped up onto the highest shelf and knocked off a box containing a pair of shoes I'd bought for a wedding and worn only once.

"Shoes?" I asked. "The clue is shoes?"

The cat meowed and, using his paw, turned the box on its side. I looked at Tara and shrugged.

"Maybe the clue isn't the shoes. Maybe it's the box," Siobhan contributed.

"The last clue on the list is TOSB," Tara contributed. "Maybe Theresa hid evidence she'd collected in a shoe box."

I frowned. "That doesn't seem very secure, and so far the other evidence has been in lockers."

"True, but there are no numbers after TOSB to indicate a locker number, so a shoe box fits."

I guessed Tara had a point. Maybe the evidence wasn't as sensitive as the other things we'd found and Theresa figured a shoe box would do. I supposed it couldn't hurt to look around Theresa's house for a shoe box full of someone's secrets.

"Okay, so say the evidence Theresa was using to blackmail TO is in a shoe box in her house. How do we get in to look for it?" I asked.

"Finn said he thought the person who vandalized the house got in through a back window. The window had a broken lock. Maybe no one has gotten around to fixing it yet and we can climb through the same way the vandals did," Siobhan said.

"Let's head over to see if we can get in," I told them. "If someone *has* fixed the window we'll just have to wait for Finn, but I'm feeling anxious to get this mystery wrapped up. We'll bring Sydney. He seems to know his way around. I'm just going to run over to the sanctuary for a cat carrier."

Luckily, by the time we arrived at Theresa's it was fairly late and most of the houses on the street were dark. The sky was clear and the moon bright, which meant we were able to find our way around the house without having to turn on our flashlights.

"Which window do you think it is?" I whispered.

"I have no idea," Siobhan answered. "Finn just mentioned that the access point seemed to be a window with a broken lock. We'll have to try them all until we find the right one."

Unfortunately, although the house was small it had quite a few windows, most of which were located behind thick hedges. I didn't want to think about what it was that was crunching under my feet as I pushed my way into the hedge to access the windows along the back of the house.

"This one seems to be locked up tightly," I informed the others before I moved down to the next window.

"Be careful," Tara cautioned. "I can hear something scampering around in the hedge. Most likely it's a squirrel you've disturbed, but you never know what might be living in that shrub."

I just hoped it wasn't something that would bite. I had on long pants, but still...

"I found it." I pushed the window open enough for me to climb through. "Go around to the back door and I'll let you in."

Once everyone was inside I let Sydney out of the carrier. He immediately began to investigate. Poor kitty must be wondering what had become of Theresa.

"I'm going to assume if she's hidden evidence in a shoe box it's located in her bedroom, so let's start there," I suggested.

"Try not to touch anything," Siobhan hissed. "I think they've already dusted for prints, but you never know when they might decide to come back for more."

"Maybe we should have worn gloves," Tara said.

"Just pull the arm of your sweatshirt down over your hand. That's what I did when I opened the door," I informed her.

I pulled the heavy drapes covering Theresa's bedroom window closed before turning on a small bedside lamp. I was pretty sure that between the fence surrounding the backyard and the drapes, no one would see the light. It didn't look like anyone had touched the room since the last time I'd been here. I headed to the closet, assuming—correctly—that that was where I'd find any shoe boxes she would have. And she had a lot of shoe boxes. At least fifty. The boxes were filled with shoes of all types, including really fancy heels, yet the only shoes I'd ever seen Theresa wear were sturdy black work shoes. Weird.

Probably about a third of the shoe boxes, which I imagined were at one time all stacked on the shelves that had been built along one wall, were already on the floor. Whoever had vandalized the house must have figured, after he'd opened twenty boxes, that shoes were all he was going to find in them and moved on. I had additional information, so I was committed to opening all the boxes until I found the one I was looking for.

As I might have predicted, the box with the clue in it was toward the bottom of the pile. It contained photographs of one of the attorneys who worked at Brown and

Bidwell in a compromising position with Bidwell's wife, Lorna. "That's Tom Osborn," I announced.

"What was he thinking?" Siobhan exclaimed. "I heard he was being considered as a third partner in Brown and Bidwell. A promotion like that would be worth a lot of money. What in the world would cause him to risk it all by messing around with the head partner's wife!"

"Lorna Bidwell is very attractive, and she's a good twenty years younger than her husband," I pointed out.

"Yeah, I guess. Still," Siobhan insisted, "the guy was an idiot to risk a partnership for a relationship that was never going to go anywhere."

"How much money do you think a partnership with Brown and Bidwell is worth?" I asked.

"Hundreds of thousands of dollars over time. Maybe more."

"No wonder Theresa was able to blackmail him. I bet he'd pay quite a lot to make sure these photos weren't circulated. I wonder how she even managed to get them. She'd have to know exactly where and when the two were going to meet."

Tara crossed the room and looked over my shoulder. The photos had been taken through the window of a motel that I was pretty sure was located on the mainland just outside of Seattle. It made sense that Tom wouldn't want to engage in an affair with his boss's wife on the island where they both lived.

"Here's the thing I'm asking myself," Tara said from her vantage point just behind me. "How did Theresa find out about the affair in the first place? Our theory is that she bugged the confessional in order to get dirt on the people she would eventually blackmail. Felicity commented about confessing to her maker, and prior to her departure from the island, she attended St. Patrick's, so that fits. Carissa attends mass regularly as well. But I've never once seen Tom set foot in St. Patrick's."

"Good point," I admitted.

"It does seem odd that Theresa would have dirt on two different people who work in the same office. Maybe she bugged the law office as well," Siobhan suggested.

"Or maybe Carissa gave Tom to Theresa," I speculated.

"Come again?" Tara looked confused.

"Here's my theory: Carissa went to confession and confessed to the embezzlement. Theresa found out after she listened to the tapes she seems to have made and decided that if Carissa was embezzling money she must have some to spare, so she decided to blackmail Carissa. We can assume the amount Theresa blackmailed Carissa for wasn't the entire amount she embezzled because Carissa has a brand-new car. A nice one. What if Carissa gave Tom to Theresa in exchange for a lighter payment? Carissa works as a secretary in the law office. Secretaries know things. Chances are she knew what Tom was up to."

"I guess that's as good a theory as any," Tara agreed.

"So what now?" Siobhan asked. "Sleeping with your boss's wife is downright rude, but it isn't against the law, so there's no need to bring Finn in on the fact that we broke into Theresa's house unless we think he's the killer."

"I guess we can try to see if he has an alibi," I mused. "If he does we can keep this to ourselves, and if he doesn't we tell Finn what we know."

"How do we get his alibi?" Tara asked.

"I'm not sure," I admitted.

"I'll talk to him," Siobhan offered. "You'd be amazed what guys are willing to tell me in exchange for a simple smile and a halfhearted compliment."

I supposed being beautiful did have its advantages.

Chapter 7

Saturday, April 23

I woke early the next morning and decided to take Max for a quick run. I was sure we'd be busy at Coffee Cat Books and I most likely wouldn't get much of a break, if any, but I felt wound up and anxious with everything that was going on in my life. Between the murder investigation, Maggie's disappearance, and Cody's uncertain future, it was a miracle I'd gotten any sleep at all.

It looked like it was going to be another beautiful day. I was more than ready for the end of winter and the arrival of spring. I tried to focus on the sound of the sea as I jogged along the sandy beach, but in spite of my best efforts, it was Cody and the decision he faced that kept returning to my mind.

I wanted to be a supportive girlfriend. I wanted to be the type of person who would put the needs of the many ahead of my own. But every time I considered my life without Cody, even for a year, I felt tension in the pit of my stomach that wouldn't quite go away.

I watched Max as he chased the seagulls who had landed on the sand ahead of us. At least he was happy and able to completely enjoy the wonder of a warm spring morning. It must be nice to be a dog and not have to worry about any moment but the present one. I supposed Max could teach me a lot about living in the now and not worrying my life away.

After I'd traveled a couple of miles down the beach, I turned around and headed back in the other direction. It would be nice if I could take the day off and simply lounge on the beach with one of the fifty-some-odd books in my to-be-read pile. It was somewhat ironic that I owned a bookstore yet rarely found the time to actually read.

As I neared my next-door neighbor, Francine Rivers's house, I noticed she'd come out onto her patio and was enjoying a cup of tea with her cats, Romeo and Juliet. I waved to her and she motioned that I should join her. I really didn't have a lot of time, but it had been a while since we'd visited, so I decided it couldn't hurt to stop for a few minutes.

"Morning, Francine."

"Would you and Max like to join the cats and me for tea? It's a beautiful morning."

"I really need to get to the bookstore on time this morning because I'm sure we'll be busy, but I guess I have a few minutes." I sat down on a patio chair across from Francine.

She poured me a cup and offered me a muffin. Max trotted over to lie down under the lounger where Romeo and Juliet were soaking up the sun.

"I heard about Theresa Lively," Francine began. "Are you investigating?"

I guess I shouldn't be surprised when my friends and neighbors assumed I'd be investigating a murder, considering the fact that I'd actually solved the previous few on the island.

"Unofficially."

"Have you spoken to Clifford Dayton?" Francine wondered.

"Should I?"

"I would. He had a pretty loud argument with Theresa on the day she died."

"Do you know what it was about?" I asked.

I love Francine. I really do. She's lived next door to my Aunt Maggie my entire life, and she's so nice and helpful to Mr. Parsons. She has a kind heart, but the woman does love to gossip, which means you have to take anything she tells you with a grain of salt. Not that she lies, exactly; it's more that she's prone to embellish.

Francine settled in to tell her story. "I stopped by the church on Wednesday afternoon to return the linens I volunteer to launder every week. When I arrived I heard Cliff and Theresa arguing. They stopped speaking as soon as they noticed my arrival, and I honestly didn't catch enough of what they were saying to be sure of what they were arguing about, but I can tell you that Cliff was plenty mad. I've never seen *anyone* turn quite that shade of red."

"You say this was on Wednesday?"

"Yes. Last Wednesday. I always return the linens on Wednesdays."

"What time on Wednesday would you say you overheard them?"

Francine considered my question. "It must have been around four. I had lunch with my garden club, which ran until one. Then I ran a few errands, picked up the linens, and headed to the church."

It sounded like the argument Francine overheard must have taken place shortly before Theresa was murdered if we were still assuming she was killed between three and five in the afternoon. At the very least if Francine had seen Theresa at four that narrowed down the window. I couldn't imagine Cliff hurting a fly, but Francine was correct in her assumption that I would want to speak to him.

I chatted with Francine for a few more minutes and then Max and I continued down the beach to my cabin. I fed him and the cats, took a quick shower, and made breakfast. I decided to call Tara while I ate. She wanted me to be at the bookstore on time because we anticipated a busy day, but I also knew she, like me, wanted this murder wrapped up as soon as possible. Once I explained the situation she agreed I should stop by the church on my way into work. Cliff worked every Saturday morning getting the church ready for the weekend services, so there was a very good chance I'd find him there.

Luckily, my assumption was correct and Cliff was happily mowing the lawn.

"Why, if it isn't Caitlin Hart. What a nice surprise on this beautiful spring morning. Something I can do for you?"

"Actually, I wanted to speak to you about something. Can you take a break for a few minutes?"

"Just let me finish this row and then we can sit on the bench near the pond and chat."

I headed over to the pond to wait for him.

Father Kilian loved to garden and he seemed to have a green thumb; the church grounds were absolutely breathtaking. I can remember hanging out at this pond when I was a kid, feeding the koi and trying to catch one of the many frogs that lived among the foliage around the crystal blue water. I sat down on one of the wooden benches that lined the water's edge and waited for Cliff to join me.

The fact that he and Theresa had been arguing seemed to give credence to the fact that whatever had happened centered at the church. Cliff was about as mild-mannered a person as you were likely to meet, so if he was yelling at the top of his lungs, as Francine had described the tone of the conversation when we spoke, it was likely he knew that Theresa had been bugging the confessional.

"Flowers are coming in right nice, don't you think?" Cliff said as he sat down next to me.

"They really are. It seems spring has been a long time in coming this year."

"Seems that way most years."

It was true. Winter did seem to hang on longer than most people liked.

I jumped right on. "I wanted to ask you about a conversation you had last Wednesday afternoon with Theresa Lively."

"Figured. Guess it can't hurt to tell what I know."

I waited while Cliff gathered his thoughts.

"I discovered on Wednesday that Theresa was responsible for what can only be described as a complete and total invasion of one of our most closely held sacraments."

"You found out she was bugging the confessional?"

Cliff looked surprised that I knew it, but he confirmed that indeed that was what he had discovered. He'd threatened to go to Father Kilian to tell him about it, which was when the argument began.

"Did you go to Father Kilian?" I asked.

"No. He'd already left and I knew he wasn't expected back until Sunday. It didn't seem right to tell anyone other than him, so I decided to keep what I knew to myself until he returned."

"Theresa was killed on church grounds not long after you spoke to her. Did you notice anyone else in the area?"

"No, not a soul. The women from the guild were there prior to my confronting

Theresa, but I knew she was planning to stay after to practice her music, so I waited to speak to her until everyone else had gone."

"And what time was that?"

"I guess around four."

"Do you know if anyone else knew what Theresa was doing?"

"To the best of my knowledge, at least one other person knew."

"Really? Who?"

"I don't know. I got a note earlier in the afternoon on Wednesday, telling me that Theresa had planted a bug in the confessional and I should look for it, so I did."

"And what time did you find the note?"

Cliff paused. He appeared to be considering my question. "It must have been around two-thirty. I know the other women from the guild had already arrived by the time I discovered it sitting on my desk and they began showing up at two."

"Do you know who left you the note?"

"No. It wasn't signed."

"Do you still have it?"

"It's in my truck."

I looked toward the parking lot where Cliff's old Ford was parked. "Can I see it?"

He agreed and we walked across the freshly cut lawn to the parked vehicle. He opened the glove box and pulled out a generic piece of white paper. with the message printed in black ink that appeared as though it could have come from pretty much any printer. I doubted it could help us, but I asked if I could give the note to Finn and he nodded.

When I left Cliff I headed back to the sanctuary to pick up the cats I planned to feature that day in the lounge and then we all headed to the bookstore. I hadn't asked Cliff for an alibi for the time of Theresa's death; I really didn't believe he had killed Theresa in spite of the extreme level of his anger. I supposed if Finn wanted to follow up with Cliff he would do so.

As I arrived at Coffee Cat Books I saw Siobhan was talking to Tara.

"So?" my sister asked.

I filled her in on my conversation with Cliff.

"Tom didn't do it either," Siobhan informed me. "He said he was at the bowling alley on Wednesday, practicing for the tournament his team is playing in this weekend. I asked the desk clerk if he remembered seeing Tom and he said he was there for a good part of the afternoon."

"The guy is an attorney. It seems like he's so busy bowling and catting around, I have to wonder if he has any time for his job. Maybe the rumors about his being considered for a partnership aren't true," I suggested.

"Oh, they were true," Siobhan verified, "with *were* being the operative word. It seems Lorna Bidwell confided in a friend about the affair she was having with Tom, who turned around and told her husband. Tom was fired a week before Theresa was killed. It seems the law firm agreed to pay him through June as long as he quietly looked for other employment off the island. They didn't want a scandal. Tom told me he has a couple of feelers out and is confident one of them will pay off. In the meantime, he's enjoying the first real time off he's had in years. He also said he told Theresa the payments he'd been sending her way had come to an end at the same time, a week before she was killed."

"So if Tom didn't do it and Carissa didn't do it, and we believe Felicity when she told me that she didn't do it, that pretty much leaves us with MH and VW," I summarized.

"Are we sure Cliff didn't follow Theresa out into the parking lot and kill her?" Tara asked. "I hate to think he would do such a thing, but he considers St. Patrick's to be his home and the parishioners to be his family, so I guess I could see him wanting to protect the church."

"I can't be a hundred percent sure he didn't do it," I said, "but my gut tells me it's not him. I'll call Finn to fill him in. I have the note to give him as well. He might want to follow up and get an alibi."

I went into the office to call Finn, who agreed to pick up the note and follow up with Cliff. When I returned to the main room of the bookstore, Miranda was there with her grandmother. I'd spoken to the woman about the idea of getting a cat for Miranda and she'd agreed that if it would help her to deal with her loss, she was all for it.

"I'm glad you could make it," I greeted them. "I brought four gentle and loving cats for you to meet today."

Miranda didn't say anything, but she did glance toward the cat lounge.

"Would you like to meet them?"

Miranda looked hesitant, but she took my hand when I offered it and followed me through the door that separated the bookstore and coffee bar and the lounge. She stood there hesitantly but didn't approach any of the cats. I noticed her scanning the room with a look of disappointment on her face."

"Do you see one that you like?" I asked.

Miranda didn't answer.

"You can pet them if you want to. The cats I brought today are all very friendly."

Miranda didn't move. She glanced at her grandmother and then headed back toward the bookstore.

"I'm sorry to have wasted your time. She really seemed to light up when Sydney jumped into her lap at choir."

"And Sydney isn't here?"

"No. He's not currently eligible for adoption. He was Theresa Lively's cat, so I guess he now belongs to her next of kin, which I assume is her daughter."

"I wasn't aware Theresa had a daughter."

"Her name is Kim. She didn't really get along with her mother. She moved to Chicago twenty years ago, and as far as I know the two never spoke again. Still, as far as I know, Kim is the only family Theresa had, so I assume she'll inherit her estate. I should ask Finn if he knows the specifics."

"It seems Miranda has her heart set on Sydney. If he does become eligible for adoption will you call me?"

"Absolutely."

Miranda and her grandmother left and I called Finn's cell, but he didn't pick up. He was most likely talking to Cliff. I left a message, asking if he had any information on Theresa's next of kin or the possible existence of a will. In my heart I knew Miranda and Sydney were meant to be together, and I was going to do everything in my power to make certain that happened.

The rest of the day flew by as the crowd we'd been expecting arrived. Tara and I were happy but exhausted as we locked the doors and reconciled the cash drawer.

"This has to be the best day we've had since Christmas," I commented as Tara counted the money.

"By far. I have to say I'm relived the sale went so well. We managed to keep up with all our bills, but just barely. If the slow season had dragged on much longer I don't know what we would have done."

"We would have figured something out," I assured my best friend.

"Yeah, I guess we would have. By the way, I was going to tell you that Lovie Bird was in today. We got to chatting about Theresa's murder and, like Carissa, she didn't seem all that upset. It almost made me wonder if she wasn't one of the five."

I thought about the codes. "None of them began with LB."

"That's true," Tara conceded. "Maybe she really is just happy that she'll finally be able to rent a locker at the bowling alley."

"A locker?"

"Lovie told me there's a waiting list and she's next in line. I guess Theresa was the owner of one of the lockers and now that she's deceased it should become available." Tara frowned. "You don't think...?"

I looked at the list. One of the codes was MHMB241-0668. "MB could stand for Madrona Bowl."

I decided to call down to the bowling alley to see if my good friend Benny King was working the counter that day. If he was I'd be able to confirm that Theresa had rented one of the lockers.

"Yep," Benny said after he answered the phone and I asked my question. "Theresa rents a locker. Or at least she did before she died. Number 241. I'm guessing someone will be by to clear out her stuff."

"Yeah, I'm sure someone will. Thanks for your help."

I hung up the phone and looked at Tara. "Locker 241 is assigned to Theresa."

"Are you going to try to access it?"

"Heck yeah."

"But you don't have the combination."

I looked at the code. "What do you want to bet the locker has one of those four digit codes and 0668 will open it?"

"I guess it's worth a try. I'd come with you, but I have a date."

"A date? With who?"

"Grant Reed."

Grant was the new leader for St. Patrick's high school group. Tara was in charge of the children's programs, so they'd worked together on a few projects.

"I knew you were friends, but I didn't know you were dating."

"We aren't. Or at least we haven't been. This is our first date. I think."

"What do you mean, 'you think'?"

"We've met to discuss the church programs, but when he asked me if I wanted to go to dinner tonight it felt different. He didn't specifically say the word *date*, but the way he asked the question felt sort of datelike."

"Dinner out on a Saturday night is most definitely a date. Have a wonderful time and don't do anything I wouldn't do."

Tara grinned. "Don't worry, I won't. It's just a first date."

"I'll fill you in on the locker situation tomorrow."

After we locked up, Tara went home to change and I headed to the bowling alley. Luckily, the place was packed with leagues, so it was easy to slip past Benny and make my way to the locker room, which I conveniently found to be deserted. Apparently my timing was good because the leagues had started a half hour earlier and everyone who had to get their equipment from their locker had already done so.

It only took me a few minutes to find locker 241 and a few seconds more to find out that 0668 did indeed open the locker. The evidence I found inside, however, would keep me reeling for the rest of the night.

Chapter 8

I returned to my cabin, let Max out for a run, and then lit a fire, poured myself a glass of wine, and considered the contents of the locker. Inside there had been a single envelope that contained a dozen photos, taken at least six months earlier. The photos showed my very own Aunt Maggie with none other than the love of her life, Michael Kilian.

The photos—which, based on the background, were taken in the fall—weren't improper, exactly, but they were intimate. One photo showed Aunt Maggie and Father Kilian walking hand in hand on the beach. He was dressed in casual jeans and a sweater and he looked so very different than he did when dressed in his priestly garb.

Another photo showed them sitting at a table looking at a photo album and laughing. There was one of them sitting side by side on a sofa looking in the direction of the camera. I suppose they could have been watching television. Although the photos were very much G-rated, anyone who saw them would come to the same conclusion I had: Maggie's mystery trips had actually been rendezvous with our local priest.

How could she? How could they?

I tucked the photos back into the envelope and wondered what I should do with them. The MH in MHMB241-0668 obviously stood for Maggie Hart. Why hadn't I seen that before? Probably because I never in a million years expected that Maggie would do something bad enough to get her blackmailed.

I looked at the photo of the codes and payments I'd taken from the ledger. It looked like Maggie had made five payments. I remembered the first time she'd disappeared, back in October, and realized that was when the photos must have been taken. The main question in my mind was why Maggie would confess to a secret getaway with Father Kilian to him. She wouldn't. Which left me to wonder how it was that Theresa knew about the meeting ahead of time so she was able to be there to get the photos. The whole thing made no sense.

After quite a bit of debate with myself I decided to hide the photos until Maggie returned and I could ask her about them. Tara would most likely ask me in the morning what had been in the locker, and I knew I'd have to lie and say it was empty, which did make me feel bad. But still...The fact that Maggie and Father Kilian had been taking off on what could only be romantic getaways would rock the entire community if word of them slipped out.

I tried to imagine what Maggie and Father Kilian were up to and why after all these years they'd decided to sneak around, but every answer I came up with was unpleasant, so I set my concerns aside and focused on something else. I did, after all, still have a murder to solve.

I had to believe that Maggie hadn't killed Theresa, which meant that if our theory was accurate and her killer was one of her victims, the killer, by default, must be VW. The question was, who was VW and where was the evidence against VW hidden?

With the exception of hiding the evidence against Tom Osborn in a shoe box, Theresa had utilized lockers around the island. We'd already discovered evidence in lockers at the high school, the community center, and the bowling alley. I tried to think about other locations in town where lockers could be found. We'd discussed the fact that the new gym had lockers, but we'd also talked about the fact that it was unlikely Theresa had had a membership. Besides, the clue was SP and the name of the gym was Bodies in Motion. It didn't seem to fit.

Being an island, Madrona didn't have a bus or train terminal. There had been employee lockers in the old cannery before Tara and I'd bought it, but we'd taken them out when we remodeled. It seemed to me that there had been lockers at the ferry terminal left over from the days when it was used to offload fish, but I was pretty sure they had been taken out as well.

I tried to remember if there were lockers at Harthaven Marina. It was still a working marina and local fishermen still docked there, so I supposed there could be lockers somewhere on the property, although I couldn't think where they'd be. The other problem was that Harthaven Marina didn't begin with the letters SP. About a decade ago there had been a restaurant on the north shore of the island named Seafood Palace, but it had burned to the ground several years ago and I doubted that lockers, if there ever had been any, would have survived.

SP. I rolled the letters around in my mind. The letter combination felt familiar, but no matter how hard I tried I couldn't think of a single place beginning with SP that might have lockers. Seal Point had an observation area, but I couldn't remember any lockers. They had put in picnic benches in an effort to create more of a parklike atmosphere, so I supposed they could have added lockers for some reason. I hadn't actually been there in years, but I could take a drive over to the east shore after lunch at my mother's the following day. If the weather held it would actually be a pleasant drive as long as my car didn't die on the way.

I looked at the two cats, who were curled up together on the sofa. They were no longer fighting, but they hadn't really done all that much to help either. I supposed Sydney had helped some, but Lucie hadn't contributed a single thing.

"Can I get a little help here?" I asked aloud.

Max barked, but the cats looked up, then went back to sleep.

I sat down on the sofa, leaned my head back, and closed my eyes. God, I was tired. I hadn't slept well since Cody had shared his upsetting news and I had a feeling a good night's sleep wasn't on the horizon until things worked their way out one way or the other. Having the investigation to focus on was helping, but even that seemed to have hit a dead end.

How hard could it be to find lockers in a location with the initials SP?

"Smith Packing," I said out loud to no one in particular. Smith Packing had been closed down for almost five years, but before it had gone under it was a large packing plant that employed quite a lot of people. It made sense that the plant would provide lockers for their employees. The plant was on the other side of the island, so it was a little late to check it out tonight. But tomorrow, tomorrow I'd take a drive to check out both Seal Point and Smith Packing. It stood to reason that one of the two locations held the final secret in the puzzle I was desperately trying to piece together.

I realized I was starving; I never had eaten lunch. I was trying to decide between cereal and takeout when my phone rang.

"Cody?"

"Yeah, it's me."

He sounded tired. More than tired. Defeated.

"Is everything okay?" Though, based on the tone of his voice, everything didn't sound okay.

"Everything is fine. I just missed you and wanted to hear your voice."

"Oh. I'm glad you called." It felt odd that Cody and I were having such a stilted conversation. We were usually so comfortable and casual with each other. "I missed you too."

"Is this not a good time?" Cody asked. Apparently he was picking up the same weird vibe I was.

"Of course it's a good time. Any time is a good time," I assured him. "I just didn't expect to hear from you until Monday. I guess when I did hear from you I was surprised, and my natural reaction was to assume that something must be wrong."

"I wasn't sure if I'd have the opportunity to call and I didn't want to make promises I couldn't keep, so I didn't bring it up when we spoke before I left. We're done for the day and it's still early, so I thought I'd call to see how you were doing. Besides, I've been going crazy not being able to see you. I guess my tendency is to worry about all the little things that could happen."

"Well, you worried for nothing. I'm great." Okay, not so great. In fact, I was totally freaked out with everything that had happened that evening, but I didn't want to worry Cody, so I kept my freak-out to myself. "How are things going with you?"

"Good. I think." I heard Cody sigh. I could picture him running his hands through his hair. "Actually, I'm not sure. The committee seems interested in my ideas, but they haven't made a formal request for me to take things further. They asked me to leave the room at the end of our session today, but they all stayed to talk, so I imagine they're discussing it among themselves and will let me know tomorrow."

"I'm sure they'll vote to follow through with your ideas. You have really good ideas. I'm sure if you want an opportunity to implement your plan they'll have no choice but to grant it."

"Yeah, I guess. To be honest, I'm not even sure if I want them to make the offer. Part of me really wants the opportunity to bring my ideas into reality and part of me just wants to go home and pick up with my old life exactly where I left off."

"Yeah, I get that. I guess I feel the same way. I want you to have the opportunity if you want it, but I don't want you to leave. I know this conversation has been awkward for some reason, but I do miss you. So much. I can't imagine not having you here every day. I guess I'm being selfish, but I want to spend all the moments of my life with you, not just a select few. On the other hand, if your plan will save lives, how can you turn down the opportunity to do whatever it is you need to do?"

Cody let out a long breath that sounded more like a sigh.

"I did bring up to the committee the fact that I'd recently purchased and updated the newspaper, and that leaving the island for any length of time would be difficult at best. I'm hoping maybe if they decide to go with my curriculum we can work out an alternative to my spending a year in Tampa."

"Do you think that's a possibility?"

"Honesty, I'm not sure. I guess my ability to bargain will depend on how badly they want to explore my idea. I really just have a wait-and-see attitude."

I wasn't sure what to say at that point, so I stayed silent. I wanted to be brave for Cody, and for my country, but at that moment I was feeling anything but brave.

"So how's your investigation going?" Cody asked to break the silence.

I filled him in on everything I'd discovered so far, except for the photos of Maggie and Father Kilian. I found I wasn't ready to share those with anyone other than Maggie herself until I understood exactly what they meant. Cody offered a few insights about the case and we exchanged ideas until we both realized we'd run out of things to consider.

"Have you talked to Mr. Parsons?"

"No," I admitted. "I've been really busy, but I thought I'd pop over there tonight to see how he's doing. In fact, I was just headed in that direction when you called."

None of that was actually true, but I wished it was because I really had meant to check in with my elderly neighbor.

"Does he know why you're out of town?" I wondered.

"I told him that I had a meeting at Kitsap, but I didn't mention the rest. I didn't want to worry him until I knew for sure what I was going to do. It's going to be hard on him if I leave."

Cody was right about that. Mr. Parsons really had grown to depend on him.

"If you do make it over it might be best if you avoid the subject altogether," Cody suggested.

"Okay, I will. We'll probably just sit together and watch reruns anyway. That seems to be what he likes to do most evenings."

"The man does like his television," Cody agreed. "I guess I should hang up so you can head over there like you planned."

"Yeah. I guess."

"I love you."

My eyes filled with tears. "I love you too."

As I promised I would, once I washed my face and got my emotions under control, Max and I headed down the beach toward Mr. Parsons's. Like Francine, Mr. Parsons had been Maggie's neighbor my entire life. The peninsula where the three neighbors lived had been divided equally between three of Madrona Island's Founding Fathers. The three large estates had been handed down from one generation to the next, and none of these founding families had sold as many of the others on the island had. The three estates were currently owned by three single people, none with children of their own, so it was hard to imagine what would happen in the next generation.

Mr. Parsons had expressed his wish that Cody take over as owner of his property when he passed. Although the property would technically leave Mr. Parsons's family for the first time in generations, Cody was a home-grown islander who would cherish the property for its intrinsic worth and not just its monetary value.

I'm not sure what Maggie intended to do with her third of the peninsula, although I'm sure she'll leave it to one of the Hart offspring. If I had to guess I'd say she'll leave her estate to either Aiden, my oldest brother, or Siobhan.

As for Francine, her husband had passed years earlier and she'd never remarried or had children, and she had no siblings, so I really had no idea where her property might end up.

I knocked on Mr. Parsons's door, then opened it just a bit. "Mr. Parsons?" I called. "It's Cait and Max. Is it okay to come in?"

I took a step inside when I didn't hear an answer. "Mr. Parsons?" I called again.

I could hear the television on in the sitting room, so perhaps he didn't hear me, though Rambler did. The dog ran down the hall to greet us, alerting Mr. Parsons to the presence of someone else in the house.

"Who's there?"

"It's Cait, Mr. Parsons."

"Well, don't lollygag; come on in."

I walked into the room, which featured not only a television turned up much too loud but the remnants of microwaved dinners. Cody made sure he ate real food when he was there; I should have come by and done so as well.

"Are you hungry? Can I make you something?" I offered.

"No, I ate. If you came by to see if I'm still alive, I am. You can go now."

I ignored Mr. Parsons, who used to be an ornery sort until Cody moved in and then became quite pleasant. His prickly disposition told me that he missed Cody as much as I did.

"Actually, I'm on my own tonight and I hate being home alone, so I thought I'd come watch television with you, if that's okay."

"Suit yourself."

"Unlike you, I haven't eaten and I'm hungry. Is it okay if I use your kitchen to scrounge something up?" I knew Cody had done the grocery shopping before he left."

"Whatever you want. Now hush; I'm missing the best part."

The movie he was watching was one I knew he'd seen at least a hundred times, but I left him to it while I went into the kitchen to cook us both a nutritious dinner and see to the dishes that hadn't been washed since Cody left.

Mr. Parsons had lived alone for most of his life, and while he was used to fending for himself, he was getting on in years and it was evident he couldn't live alone any longer. I supposed if Cody did go off to Florida for a year, we'd have to hire someone to care for him. He was going to hate that and would probably fight it, but I couldn't in good conscience leave him on his own.

I decided to whip together a beef and vegetable casserole and tidied up while it baked. When it was done I scooped it onto two plates and took them into the sitting room. I set one of the plates down in front of Mr. Parsons, who didn't say anything but did begin to eat. I poured us each a glass of milk and settled in to watch the movie.

There was something calming about sharing a meal with this man I'd known my whole life and watching a movie I'd seen so many times I could almost recite it. I'd come to visit Mr. Parsons in order to make sure he was okay, but it turned out that my visit did a lot to make sure I was okay too.

Chapter 9

Sunday, April 24

When I woke up on Sunday morning I had the sensation that the day ahead was going to be filled with shocks and surprises, not all of which were going to make me happy. Siobhan and I drove to church together, and she confirmed my fear that Maggie hadn't yet returned from her trip. When we arrived for the first mass of the day we were greeted by Father Kilian, which indicated that if they had indeed been together he had come back alone.

Because Cody was away I was left to deal with the choir on my own. At least everyone showed up on time and most of them seemed to be in a fairly cooperative mood. Luckily, Cody had lined up someone to play the piano before he went off the island. I'm not sure what I would have done if I'd been left without an assistant *and* without a pianist.

Although she didn't sing or even speak, Miranda showed up and she stood with the rest of the choir as they performed. I still needed to speak to Finn about locating

Theresa's next of kin, but if it was her daughter who had inherited her assets, as I imagined it must be, I was sure she wouldn't have any use for a cat. I hoped we could work something out so that Miranda and Sydney could be together.

Once mass was over, Siobhan and I headed to our mother's. As directed, I'd worn a dress for the occasion, in spite of the fact that it was a shorts and T-shirt kind of day. I'm not sure what I was expecting when I arrived at the house in which I'd grown up. I knew Mom had invited a guest, which was the reason she wanted us all to look nice, but I was expecting someone of the old-friend-from-high-school variety, not a fiancé none of us had ever even met.

"Engaged!" I spat after Mom announced she had plans to marry Reginald Pendergrass, the nicely dressed but much too smooth-looking man sitting next to her at the dinner table. "How can this be? When did you meet? *How* did you meet?"

"We met on the cruise the women's group I belong to went on last February."

"You've known this man for two months and you're engaged?" My mind absolutely refused to wrap itself around the idea, which I could tell everyone at the table also thought was absurd.

"Have you slept with him?" my sixteen-year-old sister Cassidy asked, a look of shock apparent on her face.

"That, my dear, is none of your business."

"Oh my God, you have. That's disgusting. I think I'm going to throw up." Cassie got up from the table and ran upstairs.

I looked around the table. Danny looked amused. He would be. I'm sure in his warped mind he was just glad the boring dinner he'd been expecting hadn't been quite so boring after all. Aiden had a guarded look on his face, but he hadn't said anything yet, which was surprising, considering he was very conservative and had taken his role of head of the family very seriously after my dad died. If anyone was going to go all ballistic, I expected it to be him.

"Do you live on the island?" Siobhan asked politely and diplomatically.

"No. I live in Newport Beach."

"California?" Siobhan's voice raised several octaves.

"Yes. On the beach. It's a very nice house with plenty of room for when you visit."

"Visit?" I asked. I looked at my mom. "You're moving?"

"Yes, dear. After the wedding."

"But you can't," I argued.

"Whyever not?"

"Because you live here. You've always lived here. *We're* all here."

"I can assure you that I'll bring your mother back to visit whenever she likes," the man told us.

I looked at my mom. "You can't be serious. This must be some sort of delayed April Fool's prank. Am I right? Please tell me I'm right!"

The monster sitting next to my mother put his arm around her shoulders and answered the questions I was throwing at her as if she was too simple to answer for herself. "Margaret and I are quite serious. We'll have a small wedding with just a few friends and family members as soon as Cassie is finished with her school year."

"You expect Cassie to move with you?" Siobhan asked.

"Of course," Mom replied. "She's my daughter and she's just sixteen."

"You can't do that to her," I argued. "She can live with me."

"Or me," Siobhan seconded.

"Cassie isn't going anywhere," Aiden finally spoke. "Nor is Mother."

I was somewhat comforted by the degree of certainty in his voice, although I wasn't sure what he could do to stop Mom if she'd made up her mind. I did notice, though, that Mom hadn't challenged him; she'd simply announced that the lasagna was ready and then asked me to fetch Cassie and Siobhan to bring the bread and salad in from the kitchen.

"Cassie," I called as I knocked on her bedroom door, "it's Cait."

"You can come in. It's open."

I turned the doorknob and stepped into Cassie's bedroom. "Are you okay?"

"No, I'm not okay," Cassie answered. "If Mom marries that man and he moves into our house I'll never be okay again. What could she possibly be thinking?"

I decided not to fill Cassie in on the fact that "that man" didn't plan to move into her home but did plan to move her into his home in another state. She had enough to worry about without adding the fear of having life as she knew it ripped away from her.

I sat down on the edge of Cassie's bed. It was obvious she'd been crying, and to be honest, I felt like crying myself.

"Has Mom seemed different to you since she's been back from her cruise?" I asked.

"I don't know. Different how?"

"Happier. More secretive?"

Cassie rolled over onto her back and looked at the ceiling. "I don't know. I'm sixteen. I have my own stuff to deal with. I try to spend the least amount of time contemplating Mom's moods as possible."

"I guess she's been lonely since I moved out and you grew up and began being away from home so often."

Cassie didn't answer at first, but she did seem to be considering my comment. "She did say something about being alone in this big old house after I go to college in a couple of years while we were taking down the Christmas stuff. I mentioned Aiden never moving out, but she had a sad look on her face."

"And then six weeks later she goes on a cruise and meets a man who wants to spend his life with her," I provided. "I guess I can see why she might be pulled in by the idea."

"But he's so old. They're both so old. Surely they can't be interested in an intimate relationship. Why can't Mom just get a roommate or move in with one of the aunts? Why does she have to marry some old guy none of us even knows?"

While I didn't agree with Cassie's assertion that Mom was too old for an intimate relationship, I did think she was jumping into this marriage thing way too fast. Not only did none of us know the guy but there was no way she could really know him herself in such a short period of time. Especially given the fact that he lived two states away.

"What are we going to do?" Cassie asked.

"I don't know, but right now Mom wants us to come down for dinner."

"Forget it. I'm not spending one minute with that home-wrecking monster. Tell Mom I'm sick."

"Are you sure? She made lasagna."

"I'm sure."

I explained to Mom that Cassie had refused to come down no matter what I said. She seemed to accept that and changed the subject to her garden club and their most recent project. Hearing about it was boring, but at least it was better than hearing about the new man in her life. As soon as dinner was over, Danny announced that he had a date, and Siobhan and I made an excuse and left as well. I imagined Aiden could handle Mom and her new boyfriend, but I did feel bad leaving Cassie behind.

"Can you believe that?" I asked Siobhan as we drove toward the peninsula.

"Not even a tiny little bit. I figured Mom would move on at some point. She's still a young woman and Dad has been gone for over five years. Still, this guy can't be for real. For one thing, Mom would never leave the island, and for another, she'd never leave us."

"So what are we going to do?"

Siobhan sighed. "I wish I knew."

She dropped me at my cabin and then headed off to Finn's. Normally, Finn came with her to Mom's for Sunday dinner, but she'd requested that only the immediate family attend this week. I guess now I knew why. I still wanted to follow up on my SP lead by visiting Seal Point and Smith Packing, so I changed into shorts, tennis shoes, and a T-shirt, checked on the cats, and then loaded Max into my car.

It was a beautiful spring day and I was looking forward to a drive around the island. In spite of the fact that Madrona wasn't all that big, it wasn't often that I visited anywhere north of Harthaven or east of Pelican Bay.

The road that hugged the coastline was heavily traveled on sunny weekends, so the trip would take several hours, but I wasn't in a hurry and wasn't all that anxious to go home to my empty cabin. I rolled down the windows, turned up the radio, and sang along with the pop rock hits of the day. There's something liberating about singing at the top of your lungs as the wind blows through your hair. If Cody were with me I'd never have the courage to sing aloud, so maybe spending a little time alone wasn't all that bad a thing after all. Of course I couldn't help but wish he would call. He'd indicated that the committee would probably fill him in on their decision today. I wasn't sure I could make it another twenty-four hours with so much uncertainty hanging over my head.

The parking lot at Seal Point was packed with visitors enjoying a day at the beach or a Sunday picnic at one of the tables that lined the bluff. I snapped Max's leash onto his collar and headed across the asphalt to the large visitor center that provided a history of the area. I hadn't been to the park since it had been remodeled and I really didn't expect to find lockers, but Seal Point did begin with SP and it was on the way to Smith Packing, so I figured I had nothing to lose by taking a look around.

As I watched the multigenerational families who had gathered to picnic, I had to acknowledge that life wasn't going to be the same if my mom did move away. The Harts had lived on the island for generations, and I guess I assumed we'd all be here for generations to come. I could remember how things had been when I was a kid and my grandparents were alive and dozens of aunts, uncles, and cousins joined us for Sunday dinner and summer picnics. Now, not only had my dad passed away but all four grandparents were gone, and most of the aunts, uncles, and cousins had moved away.

Our family might not be as large as it once was, but there were five Hart siblings, and I always figured that once we all married and had children of our own, our family get-togethers would once again take on the fullness of the gatherings I remembered.

I walked around the exterior of the visitor center and realized I wasn't going to be able to take Max inside. I could leave him in the car for the couple of minutes it would take me to go inside to check for lockers, but I hated to do that for even a minute on such a warm day. I noticed a man in blue coveralls emptying garbage cans and realized that if there were lockers on the premises he would know about them.

"Excuse me," I began. "Can you tell me if there are any lockers on the premises?"

"Not for the public."

"So there are employee lockers?"

"A few. Why?"

"A friend of mine recently passed away and I thought she might have left some of her belongings in one of the lockers here."

"Sorry, but unless your friend worked here she wouldn't have access to a locker. There are only ten, and there are more than ten employees, so they're hard to come by. I inherited locker number one from my uncle when he retired."

"So they're numbered one through ten?"

"Yup."

"Okay; thank you."

Based on the code VWSP126 I figured the locker I was looking for was most likely numbered 126. Of course it could be locker number 1, and 26 could refer to the combination, although that seemed too short.

Max and I went back to the car and continued on toward the abandoned building where Smith Packing used to be located. Before it went out of business, the company had employed dozens of people who worked around the clock on rotating shifts. It made sense that the management would have provided lockers so the men and women they employed could change at the end of their shifts.

I pulled into the gravel lot, which was completely deserted. After the cannery on the south shore of the island closed, the area had been developed by merchants such as Tara and myself, who hoped to cash in on the influx of visitors who began coming to the island once the ferry began docking on a regular basis. The north shore of the island, however, looked much as it had ten years earlier. When businesses left the area there weren't any new ones to take their place, so most of the abandoned buildings were still empty today.

While the building was large it was unimpressive. Windowless walls covered a square frame that covered more than 80 percent of the property. I wasn't sure how I was going to get in if the place was locked up, but fortunately for me, the side door hung loose on its hinges, so Max and I were able to slip in easily. Of course once we got inside it was pitch dark because there were no windows or electricity, so I returned to my car to get the emergency flashlight I kept in my glove box.

I verified that the flashlight worked, then Max and I returned to the building. Walking around in a large, dark room with the remnants of what must have at one time been functioning machinery was downright spooky. I found myself jumping at every creak and groan, which my mind tried to convince me was caused by a deranged ghost or possibly a serial killer but my common sense told me was most likely just the building settling.

I had to walk slowly so as not to trip on any of the debris on the floor. My flashlight was a powerful one that allowed me to see a large area ahead of me, which helped me to decide which direction to search first. It seemed I was in the main part of the packing plant, so it made sense that an employee lounge or locker room would be located in the rear of the large building.

Max barked as something scurried past me.

"It's just a rat, a harmless rat," I chanted to myself as my heart raced with fear and adrenaline.

I continued on one careful step at a time. When I got to the rear of the building I was happy to see that my assumption had been correct and there *was* a room with rows of lockers along one wall. The lockers were old and rusted and most of the doors hung open, which made searching for the right one quite a bit easier in spite of the fact that none of them had numbers on them. It took me quite a while to open the doors of all the lockers that were closed, so it was quite a while later that I realized all of them were empty.

"Wow, I really thought we were on to something," I said to Max.

He tilted his head, as if to convey that he was trying to understand what it was I wanted, but he clearly didn't have a clue. I rubbed my arms, which suddenly felt chilled. While it had been an exceptionally nice day, the heat of the day only lasted for a few hours, and the island evenings were still chilly. I realized I should have brought the sweater I'd worn that morning, although now that I thought about it, I'd left it in the choir room. I supposed I could stop by the church to get it on my way home.

The sun had set and it was starting to get dark by the time I arrived at the church. There was a car in the parking lot and the lights were on in the building, so I knew there was someone present on the premises. I decided to leave Max in the car; other than service dogs, animals weren't allowed inside the church. The temperature had cooled significantly from the afternoon, so I wasn't worried about the heat being too much for him.

I found Wilma Harold from the Coming Up Daisies Shop inside, refreshing the flowers. It seemed odd to me that she'd be doing that after Sunday services, but she explained that there was a baptism scheduled for the following day and the family had requested a specific type of bouquet. Now that I thought about it, there had been different flowers in the church on Wednesday than there were today. I asked Wilma how many times a week she changed out the flowers and she told me it depended on the number of special events—baptisms, funerals, weddings—for which there had been special requests.

"I'm just here to grab the sweater I left in the choir room this morning," I explained after we'd chatted for a minute.

"Cliff has already been through to clean. He usually puts any items he finds in the lost and found box in the back. Chances are that's where you'll find your sweater."

"Thanks. I'll look there first."

I headed to the little room behind the altar where the altar servers got ready for services and Father Kilian kept the robes he used for mass. Sure enough, my sweater was sitting right on top of the box marked Lost and Found. I grabbed my sweater and then noticed the row of lockers at the back of the room. I'd forgotten about the fact that lockers were provided for the altar servers' personal possessions during services. The lockers didn't have numbers on them, but they did have a piece of tape with each person's name. At the very end of the row was a locker that was marked *Lively*.

The code had been VWSP126. If VW was the blackmail victim, then SP could stand for St. Patrick's. But what about 126? It was clear each locker had a four-digit combination; 126 was only three numbers. Perhaps the combination was 0126 and Theresa hadn't bothered to write down the 0.

I tried 0126 and the door popped open. Inside was a pile of sheet music, which I removed one at a time. As I suspected I would, I found an envelope tucked in the middle of the stack. I slipped the envelope into the pocket of my sweater and returned the music to the locker before Wilma came looking for me. There'd be time enough to explore the contents of the envelope when I got back to the cabin.

The first thing I noticed when I arrived home was that Maggie's car was in the drive and the lights were on. Siobhan's car wasn't there, so I had to assume she was still with Finn. As much as I wished I could avoid the conversation I needed to have with Maggie altogether, I knew in my heart it was best to get it over with.

I took Max inside, gave him fresh food and water, checked on the cats, and then grabbed Theresa's photos and began the long walk across the lawn to Maggie's back door. I knocked once, then let myself in.

"Maggie?"

"In the living room, dear."

I walked through the kitchen, down the hall, and into the living area. "How was your trip?"

"It was nice. I only just got back a half hour ago so I still need to unpack, but I wanted to relax for a few minutes first. I was about to have a nightcap. Would you care to join me?"

"Yeah," I said. "I would. I have something I need to talk to you about."

Maggie poured two snifters of brandy and handed one to me. "Is something wrong?"

"I'm not sure." I handed Maggie the photos. "I was hoping you could tell me."

Chapter 10

Maggie looked at the photos and then back at me. "Where did you get these?"

"I found them in a locker at the bowling alley."

Maggie frowned. "Perhaps you should elaborate."

"After Theresa was found dead in her car I decided to investigate."

"Theresa's dead?"

"Yes. Since Wednesday. I figured you knew."

Maggie paled. She sat back in her chair. Her eyes looked haunted as she stared at the flames dancing in the fireplace. "No. I had no idea. I was out of contact with the outside world while I was away and, like I said, I just got back. I haven't even checked my messages yet. What happened?"

I shared with my aunt everything I knew, including the fact that Theresa had been blackmailing at least five people we knew of. I informed her that I'd found the evidence she'd stashed away on all five victims and had already identified all but the last. Then I shared with her the fact that Theresa had gotten the information she used to blackmail her victims by bugging the confessional. "What I don't get," I added, "is why you would have confessed to Father Kilian that you'd been spending time with him."

"I didn't. I'm really not sure how Theresa found out that we were meeting or how she got these photos, but I do want to assure you that nothing inappropriate has happened."

"Why don't you tell me what *has* been going on?"

"Has anyone other than you seen these photos?"

"No. I was alone when I found them and haven't shown them to anyone."

Maggie let out a long breath of relief. "I'm going to tell you what has been going on, but first you have to promise me that you won't share what I'm about to say with anyone. Not Siobhan, not Cody, not anyone."

"Okay. I promise." I braced myself for the worst. If everything was completely innocent why all the secrecy?

Maggie drank the brandy she poured herself and then refilled her glass. It seemed obvious that whatever it was she was about to tell me was difficult for her to talk about.

"I've already told you that Michael and I dated in high school," Maggie began in a voice that shook when she spoke. "I also shared with you the fact that we were very much in love and that we'd planned to marry." Maggie paused and took a breath. "Michael knew he was expected to enter the priesthood, as was the tradition with all the eldest sons in the Kilian family, but he felt such traditions were both archaic and unfair and planned to live his life on his own terms."

I knew that much. Maggie had already shared it with me after the church secretary had spilled the secret just before she tried to kill me. What I didn't know was why he'd changed his mind.

Maggie paused. It was clear she was hesitant to continue. Not that I blamed her. Confessing to an affair with the local priest, even if he wasn't yet a priest at the time, was sort of a big deal.

I decided to help things along. "So why did Father Kilian change his mind?"

"He became a priest as the result of a deal he made with God. I'm embarrassed to admit this, but shortly before I graduated from high school I found out I was pregnant with Michael's baby."

Wow. I wasn't expecting that.

"At first we were happy. We were in love and planned to marry. We'd talked about having a big family, and while we certainly didn't intend to begin it quite so soon, we found joy in the news. I'm sure if I hadn't developed complications we'd be happily married to this day."

"Complications?"

"I developed an infection that led to a high fever. I didn't want anyone to know I was pregnant, so I hid my illness from everyone for as long as I could. It was a mistake. By the time I admitted I was ill and sought medical care I was in really bad shape." Maggie paused. I decided to wait and let her finish when she was ready. A single tear slid down her cheek. "It was touch and go for a while, and though I obviously did recover, it was too late for the baby. It died and it was all my fault."

Oh, God. Poor Maggie. Poor Father Kilian.

"Anyway, as I lay in the hospital fighting for my life, Michael made a deal with God that if he spared me, he would go into the priesthood as his family expected him to do. Michael felt that my illness and the loss of the baby was a sign from God that He was displeased with us."

"Oh, Maggie, I'm so sorry. That must have been so very difficult for both of you."

"It was a very dark time in my life. I guess if there's a silver lining in all this it's that, other than the doctor and my parents, no one knew I was ever pregnant. Everyone just assumed I'd caught some strange virus. After graduation Michael went to seminary and I went on with my life as a single woman and no one was the wiser."

"And now?"

"Now we are faced with a decision. A huge decision that neither of us takes lightly. Michael has dedicated forty-five years of his life to the priesthood and he finds himself looking toward retirement."

"I guess that's natural. What's the decision?"

"Whether or not to leave the priesthood now, so that we can live out what's left of our lives together."

Oh. That *was* a big decision. "So that's why you've been meeting? To discuss it?"

"Yes. Michael feels he has kept his promise to God by spending the majority of his life in the priesthood, but now he wonders if maybe it isn't finally our time. On the surface it would seem an easy decision. Although we've kept an appropriate distance between us for the past forty-five years, neither of us has stopped loving the other. If the decision affected only the two of us, the choice to be together could be made in a heartbeat. The thing is, it doesn't just affect the two of us. There are those who wouldn't understand how a man of the cloth could ever choose to walk away from his calling. If Michael chose to do so it would affect the church, the community, and our families."

Maggie was right. A decision to leave the priesthood in order to marry would have major ramifications on the island. "What are you going to do?"

"I'm not sure. It's a huge decision and we agreed to take the time we needed to be sure we make the right choice. We did decide to spend some time together. Our weekends away have been strictly platonic. The photo of us holding hands while walking was taken in a weak moment, but I promise you that hand holding is the most intimate physical contact we've engaged in."

I believed Maggie. She looked and sounded genuine, and it was obvious she was concerned about the big picture.

"We've been spending time together because we wanted to be sure the feelings we had would stand up to the test of actually spending time together," Maggie continued. "We've maintained our friendship for all these years, but we really hadn't spent any time alone. What if Michael left the priesthood so we could be together only to find we actually annoyed each other after all this time?"

"Yeah, I get that."

"While nothing inappropriate has occurred between us, we decided it was best that we kept our trips to ourselves for the time being. I really don't know how Theresa got those photos. They're very carefully framed so that our time together looks a lot more intimate than it actually has been."

I sat back as I tried to wrap my head around everything Maggie had told me. I'd already come to terms with the fact that Maggie and Father Kilian had once dated, but a baby? Wow.

"So I assume Theresa came to you with the photos and demanded payment to keep her mouth shut."

"Basically."

"Does Father Kilian know you were being blackmailed?"

"No. And he doesn't know about the photos. Theresa agreed to keep the whole thing between the two of us if I agreed to pay her what she wanted. I really felt I had no choice. If the photos were leaked they would create chaos in the church and in the community."

Maggie's cat, Akasha, jumped into my lap as I contemplated the situation. I scratched him behind the ears as I tried to figure out my next move. I was the only one who had seen the photos, but Finn, Siobhan, Tara, and Cody had all seen the page of the notebook. The likelihood that one of them would put two and two together and realize MH stood for Maggie Hart was actually pretty good. I promised Maggie that I'd keep her secret, but I also informed her that the others had a small piece of the puzzle and that at some point she was probably going to need to come clean with the entire sleuthing team.

Maggie and I talked a while longer and then I returned to my cabin. I had a lot of information to process, but I realized that solving Theresa's murder sooner rather than later was going to work out best for everyone. I'd eliminated four of the five blackmail victims as potential killers. That just left VW.

I still needed to see what was in the envelope I'd found in the church, so I tossed a log on the fire, put on some soft jazz, poured myself a glass of wine, and curled up with Max, Sydney, and Lucie on the sofa. When I opened the envelope I found two newspaper articles that were several months old. The first showed a photo of a man and a woman standing in front of a large two-story house. The caption identified the couple as Joseph and Melanie Littlewood. The story was about the kidnapping of their ten-year-old son, Craig. According to the article, Craig had disappeared earlier that day after leaving home to make the three-block walk to the elementary school he attended.

The second article was dated a week later and claimed Melanie Littlewood had likewise disappeared from her home sometime after Joseph left to do some errands. The reporter who wrote the story speculated that perhaps Craig had never been kidnapped. It seemed the police had been called out to the house on several occasions after one of the neighbors in their upper-class neighborhood had reported shouting and other loud noises coming from the home. Though no arrests had been made, the article said it was rumored that Joseph was an abusive husband and father who might have killed his own family and reported the kidnapping to cover up his own crime.

The news clippings were tragic whatever the reason for the disappearance of Craig and Melanie, but I couldn't see how these events related to VW, or how Theresa could have used the information as leverage for blackmail. With her other victims once the evidence was discovered the who and the why had been made clear, but I had to admit in this instance I was still as stumped as ever.

I looked toward Sydney and Lucie. "I could use a little help here. How about it? Anything?"

Both cats ignored me.

I decided to call Finn. Maybe he could dig up copies of the original police reports. My hope was that there would be additional details that would make this whole thing make sense.

Finn agreed to see what he could find and then he and Siobhan would meet me at the cabin. They'd gone out to dinner, but so far my dinner had consisted of a snifter of brandy and a glass of wine, so I decided it would be best if I ate something while I waited for them to arrive.

Finn filled us in as soon as he and Siobhan settled around my dining table.

Melanie Littlewood was a financial analyst, Joseph an investment banker in

New York. According to the police interviews conducted at the time of Craig's kidnapping, they were a busy couple who each led their own lives but seemed to get along as well as could be expected given their demanding lifestyle. After Craig was born Melanie decided to stop working in order to stay home to raise her son. This decision didn't seem to cause any heartache until Joseph made a series of bad investments and lost not only a whole lot of his own money but a lot of his customers' money as well. He was fired.

Joseph was unable to get a job after several months and Melanie decided to go back to work. Craig was seven at the time so he was in school for much of the day, and Joseph took over the responsibility of childcare while Melanie worked. Based on the notes the lead detective took, it seems that was when the trouble between the couple began.

From the time Melanie went back to work right up until the day Craig was kidnapped when he was ten, there had been complaints from neighbors of loud shouting and other indications of violence such as the sound of breaking glass on several different occasions. Melanie refused to press charges so the complaints went nowhere. Three months before Craig was abducted he came to school with a black eye and a broken arm. He said he fell off his bike, but the teacher didn't believe him and called Child Protective Services. A case file was opened, but in the end, like the other times well-meaning neighbors complained, things went nowhere.

A month before Craig was kidnapped, Melanie came into the police station with multiple contusions and claimed that Joseph had beaten her up and had been doing so for years. An investigation was begun, but just like the other times, it ended up nowhere. The detective who investigated the kidnapping speculated that Joseph had friends in high places.

On the day of the kidnapping Craig walked to school as he did every other day. He never made it there. The investigator found out that there had been some trouble at home that morning and that Craig had left for school twenty minutes late, which meant that the kids he normally walked with had already gone, so he had to walk alone.

The detective in charge of the case was suspicious from the beginning, given the previous complaints from the couple's neighbors, but both parents seemed to be sincerely distressed over the disappearance of their son, and there was no evidence to suggest that anything other than what the parents reported had happened. In spite of an exhaustive search the police were unable to turn up anything. A week after Craig's abduction Joseph called 911 and reported that he'd come home from a job interview to find his wife missing and the bedroom they shared destroyed. Blood that proved to belong to Melanie was found in the bedroom, but there were no other signs of an intruder such as forced entry, unexplained fingerprints, or any other physical evidence. At that point the detective was certain Joseph had most likely killed both his son and his wife, but he was never able to find either body or any other evidence to support his theory. Joseph insisted he was innocent and even agreed to take a lie detector, which he passed. There had been no sign of Melanie or Craig in the eight months since they'd disappeared.

"Wow," I said. And here I thought Maggie's news would be the most disturbing I'd receive that night. "That's so sad either way. If Joseph was responsible for the disappearance of his wife and child he should be brought to justice, but if he's innocent I sort of feel sorry for the guy."

"Okay, so how does this relate to VW and how was Theresa using this information to blackmail someone?" Siobhan asked.

"Good question," I seconded.

"Do you think she somehow had proof that Joseph did kill his wife and child and was blackmailing him?" Siobhan asked.

"That's doubtful," Finn answered. "As far as I can tell, Joseph is still in New York and has never left. I don't see how Theresa would have had the opportunity to make contact with the man. The articles must have been stashed for another reason."

I pulled up the copy of the notebook page I kept on my computer and frowned. "The payments from VW, if we're correct in our assumption that the dollar amounts below the code are a record of payments, don't follow the same pattern as the others."

"What do you mean?" Siobhan asked.

"In every other case once the payments begin they continued right up until this month, but in the case of VW there are only two payments. One was recorded five months ago and the other a month later, but nothing after that."

"Maybe the victim refused to pay any more and Theresa decided to let it go rather than calling attention to what she was doing," Siobhan speculated.

"Maybe. But if our assumption that the killer is one of Theresa's five victims, VW must be the killer."

"What about MH?" Siobhan asked.

"Well, yeah, I guess there's that." Geez, keeping Maggie's secret while trying to solve the case wasn't going to be easy.

"So what do we do now?" Siobhan looked at Finn.

"I'm not sure. The fact that Theresa had these particular news articles hidden away is interesting, but I'm not sure how any of this can lead us to VW or the reason behind the blackmail. I guess we keep looking."

"Maybe we can figure out who MH is, and if he's the killer this VW thing will be irrelevant," Siobhan said.

"Maybe. Let's focus on that tomorrow," Finn replied before heading out.

Chapter 11

Monday, April 25

I woke on Monday morning both excited to see Cody and fearful of what he might have to tell me. I didn't know what I was going to do if he decided he needed to go to Florida for six months to a year. What would become of the newspaper? What would become of Mr. Parsons? What would become of us?

The uncertainty was making me angsty, so I decided to pull on some sweats and take Max for a walk. Perhaps I'd stop by to talk to Tansy while I was out. She'd indicated that Lucie was here to help me solve the murder, but so far she hadn't done a single thing other than hiss at Sydney.

At least it was a beautiful sunny day, perfect for a stroll along the beach. I tried to focus on the sound of my feet meeting the wet sand rather than the turmoil in my mind. I'd hoped Cody would call me yesterday after he found out what his immediate future was going to look like. The fact that he hadn't indicated to me that it was his opinion that I wasn't going to like what he had to tell me so he was waiting to do it in person. I wanted to be brave for him, but deep in my heart I just didn't know how I was going to get through this. Cody had been the one who'd wanted to speed things up in our relationship, while I was the one holding back. Suddenly I wondered why.

Max picked up a large stick and brought it to me. I tossed it into the waves as hard as I could and waited for him to fetch it. I was so ready for summer. The island definitely had several distinct personalities, ebbing and flowing with the seasons. It wouldn't be long before the whales returned and the tourist flow would expand from a trickle on the weekends to a steady flow almost every day of the week. Coffee Cat Books was only open Tuesday through Saturday during the winter, but I knew that as soon as business picked up Tara would want to open on Mondays as well.

When Max had tired himself out with our game of fetch we headed toward the dirt path that would lead us into town. It seemed I wasn't the only one on the island out enjoying the sunny morning. Several of the merchants who owned shops near the ferry were out washing windows, watering planters, and setting up sidewalk displays to encourage foot traffic to stop and take a look at what they had to offer.

I waved to several of my neighbors. Most returned my greeting with one of their own. A few even had a treat for Max when he trotted over to say hi. I was just about to turn onto the residential street where Bella and Tansy lived when I noticed a lost pet poster taped to a lamppost.

"Well, I'll be."

The flyer featured the photo of a cat named Lucie who happened to look exactly like the one back home in my cabin. The flyer offered a small reward, and at the bottom there was a phone number, address, and the name of the owner: Victoria Wilson.

"How much do you want to bet Victoria Wilson is our VW?" I said aloud to Max.

Suddenly it seemed things were beginning to fall into place. I'd take the cat home and find out what VW had to do with a blackmail scheme and a dead church pianist. If I suspected she was the killer, I'd call Finn and let him handle it from there.

Once I returned to my cabin, I had a quick bite to eat, took a shower, and secured Lucie in a cat carrier. Then I loaded her into my ancient vehicle and made the short drive into town. Finn had taken the articles I'd found; hopefully I'd be able to figure out what was going on without them.

When we arrived at the small but nicely tended home, I took Lucie out of the carrier and headed up to the front door. I rang the bell and waited. I'm pretty sure my jaw dropped when a tall woman with dark hair opened the door.

"Lucie," the woman exclaimed. She took a step toward me and gave me a huge hug as I transferred the cat into her arms. "Wherever have you been? Dillion has been worried sick."

I still hadn't said a word because, to be honest, I wasn't sure what to say.

"Thank you so much for bringing Lucie home." The woman smiled. "Please come in. Can I offer you a reward of some sort?"

I stepped into the nicely decorated home and the woman closed the door behind me.

"I don't have a lot of money," she continued, "but I do want to thank you for finding Lucie."

"Actually, she found me." I glanced around the room. My gaze settled on a photo of a boy who looked to be around ten or eleven. "You're Melanie Littlewood."

The woman paled. "No, I'm afraid you've mistaken me for someone else."

"I don't think so. Your hair is different, but I'm pretty sure you're the same woman I saw in the newspaper clippings Theresa Lively had in her locker."

"You know Theresa?"

"Knew. She was murdered."

"Yes, I heard that." The woman began to pace around the room. I could see she wanted to be anywhere but there, and I didn't blame her. Still, I did need to make sure she wasn't the killer. She didn't look like a murderer, but experience had shown that you didn't need to look like one to be one. "What are you going to do?"

"I'm not sure," I answered honestly. "Perhaps we should have a chat to see where we end up."

"Okay," she agreed.

The woman I supposed I should refer to as Victoria led me into the kitchen and indicated that I should take a seat at the table. "Does anyone else know about me?"

"No. Not yet. I didn't know myself until you opened the door. Maybe I should back up a bit." I took a few minutes to fill her in on the fact that I'd found Theresa's notebook and was using the information in it to try to track down her killer. I explained that I'd found the newspaper clippings describing the kidnapping of Craig Littlewood and the disappearance of his mother a week later. I also informed her that I'd shared my findings with the resident deputy and he'd done some research and provided a more in-depth background of the situation. The entire time I was speaking Victoria looked like she was going to throw up or pass out or both.

"I promise you I didn't kill Theresa," Victoria assured me.

"Okay; why don't you tell me what actually happened eight months ago."

"It sounds like you have a lot of the history already. Joseph and I married more out of convenience than anything. We were both professionals with busy lives and really didn't spend all that much time together. Everything was great until I became pregnant with Craig. After a lot of soul searching I decided I wanted to quit my job so I could stay home and raise my baby. Joseph wasn't thrilled with the idea, but he didn't fight me on it either. We did grow apart once I stopped working, but the real problems didn't occur until he lost his job. When he couldn't find another one right away he grew depressed and started drinking. The more he drank the meaner he got. At first it was just verbal abuse, but that led to him throwing things, and eventually he became physical with both Craig and me."

"But you never pressed charges?"

"Not at first. Joseph seemed to be sincere in his apologies after he sobered up. He promised to get counseling and to attend AA meetings, and I believed him. As time went on and things grew worse, I began to think about leaving him. When I threatened to do so he said he'd kill both of us before he let us leave, and again I believed him."

I was beginning to feel sorry for the woman sitting across from me. She'd been in a tough situation.

"Anyway, when I realized that Craig and I were in real danger, I decided I needed to take matters into my own hands. I picked Craig up on his way to school on the day he was supposedly kidnapped and left him in a safe place. I went home after I was notified he was missing and played the part of the distraught mother until I was sure Joseph believed he'd been kidnapped. I was afraid if we just disappeared together he'd know I'd left and come looking for us."

I supposed that made sense. And yet … it made me see how she might have reacted when pressed and killed her blackmailer.

"After a week I faked my own abduction. I cut myself so there would be blood in the room and vandalized the house to make it look as if a struggle had occurred."

"So how did you end up here?"

"Chance. Craig and I drove around for a few months, always heading away from New York but never really staying anywhere very long. Eventually we ended up in Seattle. I knew it was time for us to settle down somewhere. Living on an island that was isolated from the rest of the world in many ways seemed like a good idea, so we visited all the islands in the area, liked this one the best, and rented this house."

"I'm going to assume that at some point you decided to confess what you had done to a priest?"

The woman looked more than just a little shocked. "Yes. How did you know?"

"Theresa bugged the confessional. That's how she targeted her victims."

"I should have known. I'd never told anyone who I really was, and I knew Craig wouldn't either. I wanted a fresh start when we settled here, so I decided to tell the only person who I knew would keep my secret. I guess that was a mistake."

"I'm curious about your payments to Theresa. There were only two and then they stopped."

"I don't have much money and I told her that. I managed to scrape up the first two payments, but no matter how hard I tried I couldn't get the third. Theresa said she'd once been a battered child and felt sorry for me. She gave me back the money I'd already paid and told me she would keep my secret."

I supposed Theresa having been a battered child could explain quite a lot, actually.

"What are you going to do?" Victoria asked. "Are you going to turn me in?"

"No," I decided. "I believe you didn't kill Theresa, and as far as the fake kidnapping goes, I imagine I would have done the same thing in your place. The resident deputy is a smart guy; he might figure things out on his own, but I doubt he'll do anything to disrupt the life you're trying to build here."

Victoria got up from her chair, came around the table, and hugged me. "Thank you. Dillon really likes it here. I'd hate to have to move again."

I chatted with Victoria for a few more minutes and then returned to my cabin. Cody had promised to come by as soon as he arrived on the island and I wanted be sure I was there with welcoming arms and an open mind. Or at least as open a mind as I could muster.

By the time Cody arrived I was a nervous wreck. I really wanted to be cool, calm, and collected, but the more I considered the possibility that he might be leaving, the more freaked out I became. When Cody pulled up in front of the cabin I ran outside and threw myself into his arms. His lips met mine and he lifted me up and carried me inside. It was quite a while before we actually got a chance to talk.

"So how'd it go?" I really hated to ask, but I did need to know.

"Good."

Good? What did that mean? Good as in they loved his ideas and he'd be heading to Florida, or good as in they hated them and he'd be staying here on Madrona Island?

Cody must have realized I was asking for more details because he continued without my prodding. "They loved my ideas and they agreed that, with a few alterations, they would improve the current training program."

My heart sank. He was leaving.

"They also understood that I'm a civilian now and I've built a life here on Madrona Island, so leaving for an extended period of time was a lot to ask."

Okay; this was sounding better. "So?"

"So we worked out a compromise. I'm going to write the new curriculum with input from key individuals they'll put me in contact with, but I'll do it from Madrona Island in my spare time."

"You're staying?"

"I'm staying. Well, mostly."

"Mostly?"

"I did agree to a few short trips to Tampa as the program is created, but we're looking at a week at a time at the most."

A week sounded doable. I could live with that. "So tell me about the program." Now that I knew Cody wasn't leaving I was excited to hear what he'd planned.

When we'd exhausted the subject of Cody's training program the conversation worked its way around to the murder I'd been investigating in his absence. "I was really sure one of the five people Theresa was blackmailing was the killer, but now that I've spoken to all of them I'm not so sure. Felicity was picked up by the police in Seattle after Finn forwarded her information to them. She admitted to her involvement in the accident that killed the old man but is insisting she didn't kill Theresa. She even volunteered to take a polygraph. At the time of the murder Carissa was at a softball game on Orcas Island, Tom was at the bowling alley, and while I can't discuss the identities of the other two because I promised not to, I'm certain neither is the killer."

"Let's take a look at the video of Felicity arguing with Theresa," Cody suggested. "Maybe we can pick up a detail that was missed before."

I pulled the video up on my computer. The first time I'd watched it I'd been focused on the conversation between the two, but now I noticed other details. For one thing, there was a clock in the background that said the time was one forty-two. I remembered Cliff saying that he'd discovered the note on his desk at around two-thirty, and that the women from the guild had shown up at around two. Theresa must have arrived at the church prior to the meeting to speak to Felicity. I guess that made sense. I had no idea why they'd chosen to meet in the church. There must have been other locations that would have provided more privacy.

"Who do you think was taping this?" Cody asked.

"I don't know. That's a good question."

"If one of the five blackmail victims isn't the killer, maybe the person recording the video is."

"Is there a way to backtrack and find out where the video was sent from?" I wondered.

Cody sat back and looked at me. "Maybe. It depends on how tech savvy the person who sent the video is." Cody pulled the computer over so it was in front of him. "Let me see what I can find out."

I waited while Cody punched in commands. It wasn't like he was a cyber genius, but he definitely knew his way around a computer a lot better than pretty much anyone else I knew.

"That's interesting," Cody said.

"What's interesting?"

"The video was sent from one of the computers on the church network."

"Which one?"

Cody continued to type, exposing rows of code that meant nothing to me. "I'm not a hundred percent sure, but I'm going to guess it's the one in Father Kilian's office. Why would Father Kilian send you this video?"

"He wouldn't. Besides, he wasn't there that day."

"Are you sure?"

"I'm sure. His office wasn't locked. Remember, I went in to get the envelope with the notes he wanted me to present at the community dinner meeting."

"So someone taped the argument and then sent it to you?"

I frowned. "No. At least they didn't send it to me at the time of the argument. I didn't receive it until the next day. Whoever sent it must have regular access to the church building. Let's play the tape again."

Cody agreed and the scene unfolded once again. I tried to notice any small detail that might lead to a clue. It seemed obvious that neither Theresa nor Felicity was aware of the person taping their argument. Neither glanced in the direction of the person behind the camera at any point.

"Do you think this was recorded with a cell phone?"

"Probably," Cody responded.

"Based on the vantage point, it looks like the person making the recording was in the room behind the altar. What if it wasn't planned? What if someone happened to be in that room for some reason? Theresa and Felicity came in and started arguing. The person in the room realized it was significant, so they recorded it."

"I guess that's as good a theory as any."

"So who would be in the church at that time of day? The women from the guild didn't show up until two."

"Maybe one of them was early."

I supposed we could find out who'd been there that day and then ask them who might have been early. If someone was there Felicity might have seen another car in the parking lot when she arrived. I wondered if she might remember what the car looked like. Of course given the fact that she'd left the island and I didn't have her contact information, it might be difficult to call her up to ask.

Cliff was on the premises that day, I realized. Maybe he would remember who was there before two o'clock.

"Cliff said he was left a note that prompted him to look for the bug," I informed Cody. "He said he found the note at around two-thirty but waited to confront Theresa until four because he wanted to wait until the other women left and he knew she would stay behind to practice the piano. What if the person taping the argument between Theresa and Felicity is the person who left the note?"

"Then he or she would most likely have used one of the computers in the church."

"Maybe the person doing the taping had confronted Theresa, or Theresa realized someone was there. She confronted that person, was killed in the altercation, and the killer used her keys to put her into the trunk of her car. Then she took the car to Theresa's house and parked it in the garage. But why lock Sydney in the confessional, and why trash the house?"

"Maybe Theresa had some sort of evidence on someone other than the five people in the notebook. The killer could have been looking for it."

"Still, that doesn't explain the cat." I looked at the tape one more time. "The flowers."

"What about the flowers?"

"They were peach on the Sunday before Theresa was murdered. I remember that because they matched Annabelle's dress. The flowers in the background were pink and white. At least some of them were." I pointed to the screen. "The flowers on the left side of the altar are still peach, but the ones on the right are pink and white."

Cody looked at me. "So?"

"So Wilma told me that she changes out the flowers several times a week if there's been a request for a special event. I'm going to go out on a limb and say that Wilma was in the church making the change when Theresa and Felicity arrived."

Cody appeared to be considering my theory. "Okay, so why did she hide in the back room when they came in?"

"Maybe she didn't. Maybe she was back there anyway for some reason. There are lockers back there. If she changes the flowers as often as she indicated, maybe she keeps some supplies on site in case she needs them."

"Sounds like I need to buy you some flowers."

"Sounds like maybe you do."

Cody and I headed into Harthaven, where Coming Up Daisies was located. If Wilma had witnessed the fight between Theresa and Felicity, maybe she had additional information as to exactly what had occurred.

The flower shop was a bright and sunny storefront that was decorated in cheerful colors that helped to accentuate the artfully displayed flowers that greeted visitors with a heavenly scent.

"Cait, Cody, how nice to see you," Wilma greeted us. "What can I do for you today?"

Cody crossed the store to look at a basket of flowers while I approached Wilma. We'd decided I would talk to her alone so she wouldn't feel like she was being ganged up on. "Actually, I just wanted to talk to you for a few minutes, if that's okay."

"Sure. As long as no customers come in."

"I guess you heard about Theresa," I began.

"Yes, I heard."

"Someone tipped Cliff off that Theresa was bugging the confessionals. I thought it might have been you."

Wilma didn't answer right away.

"I hate to put you on the spot, but I really need to try to understand the sequence of events on the day Theresa died."

"You think I killed her?"

"Did you?"

"Of course not. I was at the church changing the flowers for a wedding the following day. The bride and groom had arranged to have her uncle, who's a retired priest, perform the ceremony and Father Kilian agreed to let them use St. Patrick's."

I waited silently for her to continue.

"I was in the back room, using the counter to trim the ends of one of the displays, when Theresa and Felicity came in from the hall. They were arguing. I didn't want to interrupt them; it seemed to be an emotional discussion, so I waited in the back for them to finish. At some point I realized the argument wasn't just emotional but potentially deadly. I decided to use my phone to record what I could without giving my presence away. To this day I wonder if I should have interrupted, but at the time I was scared. Felicity wasn't just mad; she was enraged. After she left Theresa went over to the confessional and took something out of it. I realized it must be a device used to record conversations. Suddenly everything I'd heard made sense. I remained hidden until Theresa left to meet the other women who were arriving for the meeting. When I figured I was safe I finished up with the flowers, loaded my van, and then headed down the hall to Father Kilian's office to type out a note revealing that Theresa had bugged the confessional. I left it on Cliff's desk and headed back into town."

"Why did you do that?"

"I wanted Theresa to be caught, but I didn't want to be the one to confront her. I knew if Cliff found out what was going on he'd put a stop to it."

"Do you think he did? Put a stop to it?"

"Cliff? Why, no. Cliff wouldn't hurt a fly. He's protective of the church and has a pretty loud bark, but I don't think he has much of a bite, if you know what I mean."

I did.

"And the tape you sent to Felicia and me?"

"I wasn't going to send the tape until I realized Theresa was dead. I decided I needed to make public what I knew, so I came back to the church and used Father Kilian's office to send the video. I knew you were something of an amateur sleuth, so I figured you'd know what to do with it."

I supposed that made sense, but I wondered why she'd sent a copy to Felicia too. I asked that very question.

"I don't know. I guess it seemed like a good idea at the time, but looking back, it might have been better not to tip her off. I heard she left the island before she could be arrested."

"She was picked up by the Seattle PD."

Wilma let out a long breath. "Good. I hated to think I was responsible for letting her get away."

"When you left the church did you notice who else was on the property?"

"There were a few cars. Theresa's of course, and two others. I'm not really sure what type of vehicles the other members of the women's group drive, but there was a dark blue Ford, a four-door, and a white van. I'm not sure of the make and model."

"Okay, thank you. And please do call me if you think of anything else that might help us figure out who killed Theresa."

Cody and I headed back toward the peninsula after he bought two bouquets, one for me and one for Francine, who had looked in on Mr. Parsons while he was away.

"So if one of the blackmail victims didn't kill Theresa and Wilma didn't do it, who are we left with?" Cody queried.

I wasn't sure. Cody and I had arrived at the church at five and the parking lot had been empty. Cliff had said he'd argued with Theresa at around four and then she left. If she was killed in the parking lot, it must have happened right after arguing with Cliff. You would think someone would have seen something, but it had been a rainy and dreary day so there hadn't been a lot of people out and about. Besides, the parking lot was behind the church and therefore not visible from the street. It seemed we were running out of suspects.

Unless..."Okay, how is this for a theory: When I ran into Felicity on the ferry she said she was on the way to the island to take care of some business that couldn't wait. That was on Tuesday. We know she met with Theresa on Wednesday at around one-thirty. Here's the thing: If you listen to the tape of her confession, she said *we* were just messing around and *we* didn't see him until it was too late."

"So there were other people in the car," Cody realized. "I wonder why only Felicity was being blackmailed."

"Maybe Theresa didn't know who Felicity was with. She never really said, and maybe she never did tell Theresa. So Felicity decided she was done making payments to Theresa. She realized that if Theresa spilled her secret it could also affect the other person or persons in the car, so she called them and gave them a heads up that if there ever were an investigation it could end up revealing the identities of everyone involved. Maybe the other half of Felicity's *we* wasn't willing to risk that, or taking over the blackmail payments, so they decided to kill Theresa."

"Okay, so how do we find out who Felicity was with?"

"I guess we fill Finn in on our theory and hope he can get her to talk.

Chapter 12

Wednesday, April 27

Finn hadn't been successful in his bid to get Felicity to share who she'd been with in the car. I had to wonder who it was she was protecting that she was willing to turn down a chance at a lighter sentence if she agreed to roll over on her car mate. In a strange sort of way, I almost admired her willingness to protect the person who obviously had been a friend, at least at the time. Felicity had been in Siobhan's class; maybe my sister remembered who Felicity had been closest to in high school. It couldn't hurt to ask. At least she might be able to provide a starting point.

Siobhan had stayed over at Finn's the night before and I had to get to work, so my chat with my sister would have to wait. In the meantime, I decided to follow up on a few other ideas. I'd remembered that Felicity had dated a guy named Brad Jones for a while after graduation. I couldn't remember whether they were still together up to the point when she moved off the island, but Brad still lived on Madrona and worked at the fish market just down the street from Coffee Cat Books. If I had a free moment I'd head over to see what, if anything, I could find out.

Luckily, Destiny was working a full day, so after the crowd from the first ferry cleared out Tara thought it would be fine for me to take a short break for an interview.

"Halibut is fresh," Brad greeted me.

My intention hadn't been to buy fish, but I did love halibut. "I'm working today, but if you can set some aside for me I'll stop back at the end of the day to buy two filets."

"Done. Anything else while I'm at it?"

"Maybe a dozen prawns and a tub of your special cocktail sauce." Cody was coming by for dinner after choir tonight and a home-cooked dinner of fresh seafood would be just the thing to set a romantic mood. "I ran into Felicity when she was here last week."

"Yeah, she stopped by. It was good to see her."

"I seem to remember the two of you used to date."

"For a while. Before I met Olivia. We had a bad breakup, but after Olivia and I got together we ran into each other and we realized we were never really meant for each other."

I knew Brad had married his wife only a year ago, so it was possible he was dating Felicity at the time of the car accident. I needed to figure out a way to explore that question without seeming obvious. If he'd been involved in the accident a direct question about the night a man had been killed was only going to tip him off that Felicity had talked.

"It's nice when exes can be friends. Felicity seems to be doing well in Seattle, and you and Olivia seem very happy. I guess everything really did work out for the best."

"It definitely worked out for the best for me. Felicity was a wild one when we were together. I might have ended up in a totally different place if I'd stayed with her. Luckily, I was able to see that she was going to get me into trouble eventually and broke things off before it was too late."

"I seem to remember hearing something about some pretty wild parties," I fished.

"The wildest. Felicity used to hang out with Darcy North, and Darcy was famous for throwing totally insane parties. In fact, it was at one of those parties that I decided to end things. It was hard at the time because I was really in to Felicity, and she took it hard, which made me feel bad. But she moved away not long after that, and things got easier. Looking back, though, it was the right thing to do. I have a wonderful wife with a baby on the way."

"A baby? I hadn't heard. Congratulations."

"Thank you; we're very happy."

Another customer walked in, so I promised to be back later for my order and returned to the bookstore. It didn't seem like Brad was the person I was looking for. I'd watched his face as he spoke and he'd never appeared guarded. It seemed things probably had gone down exactly as he'd said. He did give me a new lead, however: Darcy North. I did remember she'd gone through a wild period, although she seemed to have calmed down after she became a single mother.

Darcy worked as a receptionist at a dentist's office in Harthaven. It wouldn't be as convenient to drop by to talk to her, but I was sure Tara wouldn't mind as long as the bookstore wasn't too busy. The next ferry was due in half an hour, so maybe after that crowd cleared out.

"Actually, that would work out great," Tara responded when I broached the subject. "I have an order I promised to deliver to the hygienist in the office. You can drop it off for me."

"That's perfect. It even gives me a reason to be there. I was afraid I might actually have to make a dental appointment."

It was another beautiful spring day and I enjoyed the fact that I was able to get out of the shop and take a drive. It didn't take all that long to make the trip from Pelican Bay, where Coffee Cat Books was located, to Harthaven, but I rolled down the windows and enjoyed every minute of the journey.

Luckily, the reception area was deserted when I arrived. Darcy smiled as I approached the desk.

"Is it time for your cleaning already?"

"Actually, no," I answered. "I'm just here to drop off an order for one of the hygienists."

"Oh, okay. I'll be sure she gets it."

"By the way, I ran into Felicity the other day. It was good to see her. I remember the two of you were friends."

"Yeah, we were. Back in my wild and crazy pre-mom days. I haven't seen her for years. Did it seem like she's doing good?"

"She said she has a busy life in Seattle," I answered vaguely.

"That's good. She seemed to be in a pretty dark place after she broke up with Brad Jones. I'm glad things worked out for her."

"It's funny you should say that. I just spoke to Brad today. I stopped by to buy some halibut, and he mentioned that Felicity had stopped by to see him when she was on the island recently. I guess they managed to retain their friendship."

"That's kind of amazing. He was so mad that night when Felicity and I left a party with Cora and some of the others. I wasn't at all surprised he broke up with her the next day."

"That must have been the Christmas party you had at your place?" I fished.

"No, before that, at the post-Halloween freaks and geeks party."

"The one you used to hold every year on the weekend after Halloween?"

"Yeah. That would be the one. Talk about a wild time. Sometimes I miss that wild and crazy time in my life, but then I look at my adorable little boy and realize I wouldn't trade him for anything."

Darcy looked up. "It looks like our next appointment is here. I'll be sure the hygienist gets this."

After I left I called Finn to verify that the night of the freaks and geeks party Darcy had referred to was the same one on which the man had been run off the road. It was. If Darcy had been in the car that night, it was odd that she was able to speak so comfortably about it. Maybe the accident had occurred after she was dropped off. Either that or she had an awesome poker face. She had specifically mentioned that Cora was one of the people Felicity had left the party with. I assumed she was referring to Cora Belmont, who conveniently worked at the grocer just down the street. I wanted to pick up ingredients for a salad to have with our dinner that night, so a trip to the market seemed like a logical stop.

My conversation with Cora was brief because she was working the meat counter. I was able to confirm that she was one of the girls who left the party with Felicity, who had been driving, and was the last one to be dropped off. She said Felicity had been heading over to some guy's house who gave her the creeps, so she'd asked to go home. I asked his name and she said he went by Ringo. He was quite a bit older than they were, and while she didn't know his real name, she did know he played in a band.

Now all I had to do was track down Ringo. By the time Cora had been dropped off it was well past midnight. Chances were this guy was the person who was in the car with Felicity when the man had been run off the road.

"We have a lot of songs to get through tonight so I need everyone to focus," I said to the children that evening.

"Are we going to practice that new song you've been talking about all month?" Annabelle asked.

Were we? I wasn't sure. The substitute pianist Cody had arranged to play for the choir last Sunday couldn't do it on a permanent basis, so we were without accompaniment tonight. The kids did fine practicing the songs they knew without the piano, but I wasn't sure how they'd do with a new song if they couldn't hear the melody.

"I think we might want to wait until we can find someone to play the piano," I answered.

"Can't you do it?"

"I can get by, but I'm not really very good. I'm afraid I might mess you up if my pacing is off."

"So get Mr. Dayton to do it," Annabelle suggested. "He's cleaning the church. I saw him."

"Mr. Dayton the janitor?"

"Yeah. He used to be in a band. My dad told me he knows how to play lots of instruments."

I frowned. Cliff was in a band? Surely Cliff wasn't Ringo? Cora had indicated that the man Felicity was going to meet was a lot older than she was, and if he really was Ringo and realized Theresa knew his secret, that could account for the intensity of his anger.

Suddenly I had a bad feeling.

"That's a good idea," I said. "I'll just run down the hall to get him. If Cody gets here, tell him where I went."

I called Finn as soon as I got into the hall and away from little ears. I told him my suspicion and he said he was on his way over and that I should return to the choir room and not approach Cliff. I decided that was a good idea and was about to do just that when someone approached from behind me and put a hand over my mouth.

"Who were you talking to?" a deep voice I knew belonged to Cliff said.

I pointed to the hand over my mouth to indicate that I couldn't answer unless he removed it.

"I'm going to take away my hand, but if you scream or make any sort of noise we're going to have a problem. Do you understand?"

I nodded my head.

Cliff slowly removed his hand. "Who were you talking to?"

I didn't want to tell him that Finn was on his way. I was afraid it would create a hostage situation. I tried to consider exactly what Cliff could have heard from only my side of the conversation. When Finn had answered I'd said I thought Cliff was Ringo. We'd already discussed the fact that Ringo was most likely the person Felicity was with in the car and quite likely Theresa's killer in a previous conversation, so I hadn't needed to say that.

"I was talking to Cody," I lied. "We've been trying to figure out who to get to take over as the new pianist and someone told me there was a man in town named Ringo who used to be in a band. The problem was, we didn't know Ringo's real name, but one of the kids just filled us in. I was going to come down the hall to ask if you would play for us tonight. What's with the cloak-and-dagger stuff?"

"You're lying."

"I'm not lying. Why would I lie?"

Cliff grabbed my hand. "How about we take this outside? I wouldn't want to disturb the kids."

I couldn't agree more. The last thing I wanted to do was to get the kids involved. The farther I could get Cliff from the roomful of kids the better, so I let him lead me into the dark night. I hoped he'd stop and we could talk in the parking lot because Finn would be there any minute, but he kept walking until we reached the gardening shed. He opened the door and shoved me inside. The shed had no windows, but it did have a small light. He turned it on, casting an eerie glow inside. I knew Finn would come looking for me, so all I really needed to do was keep Cliff talking and hope he didn't decide to deal with me the same way he had Theresa until Finn got there.

"Would you mind telling me what this is all about?" I asked.

"I think you know."

"Know what?"

A slight look of doubt came over Cliff's face. "You've been investigating Theresa's death."

"Yeah. So? I already spoke to you. Did you have something to add?"

My heart was pounding, although I tried to play it cool. I couldn't let him sense my fear. I had to make him think I was as confused as I was trying to appear.

"Where did you hear about Ringo?" Cliff asked.

"I don't know. Someone mentioned him to Cody. He's been asking around, looking for someone to take over for Theresa. Some guy he met in a bar said there was a local guy who could pound out a melody like no one else. He said he hadn't heard him play for a while, but he thought he was still around. He said he went by Ringo, but he didn't know his last name, and he didn't even know whether Ringo was the guy's real first name. Why didn't you tell me you could play the piano? You know we've been looking for someone."

The look of doubt and confusion on Cliff's face seemed to deepen. I could tell he was considering what I was telling him.

"So who told you I was Ringo?"

"One of the kids. The kids wanted to rehearse a new song, but I didn't think we could do it without a piano. One of the kids said to ask you, that you played the piano really well. He said his dad told him you used to be in a band. I was heading down the hall to talk to you when Cody called to say he was going to be late, so I told him that I thought you might be Ringo."

Cliff didn't say anything.

"Now that I've answered your questions, would you mind telling me why you dragged me out here?"

I hoped my voice held just the right amount of indignation. If I didn't know what was really going on and I really had been simply coming to ask Cliff to play for us, I would have had a high level of indignation in my voice.

Cliff didn't answer. He just stared at me. I could hear a car pull into the parking lot. I hoped it was Finn, although it could have been Cody arriving late. Either way, someone would be looking for me very shortly.

"Is it okay if I return to practice now?" I asked. "Cody's late tonight, so the kids are in the choir room without supervision. You know if I don't get back soon they're going to make a mess."

"Did you ever figure out who killed Theresa?" Cliff asked.

"Actually, we did. It turns out it was one of her blackmail victims. A woman named Nina Gold." I made up the first name that came to mind.

"Did she confess?"

"No. But Finn thinks he has a good case against her. Can we go back inside now? It's freezing out here."

Cliff seemed to relax. "Yeah. We can go inside. Sorry I was a little rough."

"No problem. So what do you think about the choir gig? Are you in?"

Cliff opened the door to the shed. I stepped outside. He stepped out behind me. I thought I'd averted a crisis until Cliff noticed Finn's car in the parking lot.

"I knew you were lying." He grabbed my hair and pulled me back against his body.

"Finn!" I yelled as loudly as I could.

The next few seconds seemed to pass in slow motion. Cliff slapped me. Finn appeared from the parking lot with his gun drawn. Cliff pulled out a knife and threatened to slit my throat, there was the sound of a gunshot, and then Cliff fell to the ground.

"Is he dead?" I asked.

Finn felt for a pulse. "No, he'll live. Run inside and call 911. Tell them to send an ambulance. I'm afraid I dropped my radio when you screamed."

I ran over and hugged Finn. "Thank you."

"Any time, little sis."

"Wow, that's quite some story," Siobhan said later that evening. Cody had shown up shortly after Finn arrived. We'd called all the parents and had the kids picked up early and then the two of us returned to my cabin while Finn saw to booking Cliff. "I still can't believe Cliff killed Theresa. He seems like such a pussycat."

"I guess when he found out that Theresa had been bugging the confessionals he realized she knew Felicity's secret and she'd eventually find out he was involved as well. They were alone at the church between the women's group leaving and Cody and me arriving, so he killed her, put her in the trunk of her car, and drove her home."

"He must have trashed her house looking for any evidence she might have regarding the car accident. What I don't get is why he put Sydney in the confessional."

"That's the weird thing. He swears he didn't."

"So who did it?" Siobhan asked.

"I have no idea. I suppose we may never know."

"I don't get why Felicity was protecting Cliff," Siobhan said, wondering the same thing that had gone through my mind more than once. I just assumed her partner in crime was someone she cared enough about to protect. I doubted she cared about Cliff one way or another.

"I think I can answer that," Cody said as he joined us. He'd been on the phone while we were chatting. "It seems Felicity was pregnant on the night of the accident."

"With Brad's baby?" I wondered.

"With Brad's baby. She said she was stupid and told Cliff, and then, the next day, she realized she didn't want Brad to know about the baby, so she made a deal with him that she would never tell anyone that he was actually the one driving if he didn't tell anyone about the baby."

I frowned. "Felicity has a baby?"

"She gave her up for adoption. She knew Brad would never agree to the adoption, so she never told him about the baby. She faked the identity of the father on the adoption paperwork, but Cliff knew the truth and she was afraid he would tell Brad. I suppose Brad could have had some rights in the situation. I guess she didn't want to risk it."

"So she was willing to go to jail? Her sentence would have been greatly reduced if she had given up Cliff."

"The baby was adopted by a friend of hers. She's an honorary aunt and gets to see her daughter all the time. She couldn't risk Brad messing up the life she'd given her child."

I guess that made sense. She wasn't really protecting Cliff; she was protecting her baby. I had to wonder what would happen to that child when Brad was informed that he had a daughter he'd never known about.

Chapter 13

Friday, April 28

Now that Theresa's killer had been caught I knew it was time to find a permanent home for Sydney. Finn had informed me that he'd spoken to Theresa's daughter, who'd confirmed she didn't want the cat, so I was free to do with it what I pleased. I called Miranda's grandmother, who was still interested in adopting Sydney as long as Miranda and Sydney continued to demonstrate the bond they'd shown that first day in the choir room. I made arrangements to bring him by after Miranda got home from school.

Miranda's grandmother lived in a small house in Harthaven. It was a nice, older neighborhood, and most of the residents had lived there for quite some time, so they tended to be seniors like her. I felt bad that there weren't other children in the area for Miranda to play with, but I understood the grandmother couldn't just up and move after all this time.

Miranda opened the door when I knocked. She smiled when she saw me holding Sydney.

"Is it okay if I come in?"

Miranda stepped to the side.

I set Sydney down on the floor and he immediately ran to where Miranda was standing. She dropped to the floor and began to pet him.

"It seems," I began after Miranda's grandmother joined us, "that Sydney is in need of a new home. I don't suppose you know anyone who would be interested in adopting a cat?"

Miranda looked at her grandmother, a look of longing on her face.

"I guess you need to be sure he goes to a home where there's someone who will take good care of him," Grandma responded.

"Yes. Someone to take care of him will be very important."

"I can take care of him," Miranda said aloud.

I noticed tears forming in the corners of Grandma's eyes. She struggled to control them, I imagined for Miranda's sake. "I guess we could work something out with Miss Cait if you're sure. It's a big commitment."

"I'm sure. I'll take good care of him. I promise."

"Well, okay. If you're sure."

Grandma looked at me.

I glanced at Miranda. "I guess if you promise to take very good care of him I can let you adopt him."

"Oh, I will." Miranda looked at her grandmother. "Can he sleep in my room?"

"If you'd like."

"Come on, Sydney." Miranda picked up the cat and started down the hall. "I'll show you where you're going to sleep. It's scary when your mom dies and you have to move to a new house, but I'll be your new mom. I think you'll like it here."

It took everything in my power not to start bawling myself. I really loved it when one of the cats in my care found its perfect match.

"That's the first time Miranda has spoken since her parents' death," Grandma shared after Miranda went into her room. "I was beginning to fear her inability to speak was going to be permanent. It's been such a long time."

I could hear Miranda in the distance, chatting with the cat. "I guess she was just waiting to have something important to say."

"Yes." Grandma smiled. "I guess that was it all along."

After I left Miranda's I headed back to the peninsula. I was exhausted after everything that had happened in the past week, so Tara suggested I take the afternoon off. Destiny was there to help her, and the two of them planned to begin training a new part-time employee to help out with the summer crowd. When I arrived at the cabin I noticed Maggie out tending her rose garden.

"Seeing you in the garden has confirmed my suspicion that spring is finally here."

Maggie sat back on her knees and smiled. "I do love this time of year, when everything that's been dormant is reborn and the world is alive with color."

"Seems like you're in a good mood." I knelt down beside her and began to pull at random weeds that were just starting to poke through the rich soil.

"I am." Maggie wiped a hair off her face, leaving a smudge of dirt across her cheek. "In fact, I think this is one of the best moods I've been in for quite some time. I feel as light as a butterfly."

"Any particular reason for the lift in spirits?" I wondered. "Other than the chance to get out in the garden, that is."

"I decided to tell Siobhan my secret."

I had to admit that surprised me.

"It didn't seem right to ask you to keep such a big secret from your own sister. I was nervous at first, but she seemed to understand, and she's promised to keep my secret until an announcement can be made."

"An announcement?"

"Michael has decided to retire after the end of the year."

"And...?"

"And we agreed that once a replacement is found and put into place we'll give it six months, maybe more, before he announces his plan to leave the priesthood."

"So you're going to do it? You're finally going to be together?"

"Yes." Maggie smiled. "We finally are. In the meantime, we agreed not to spend time together outside of church and family events. Our trips away have accomplished what they were intended to. Anything more would be self-indulgent."

"Wow. If you wait until a replacement is found and settled in, you could be looking at two years. Maybe more."

"It's the right thing to do, and we can wait."

I remembered a saying I'd read. I couldn't remember where, maybe in a book. But it seemed to sum up the love affair between Maggie and Michael Kilian exactly:

Love in its purest form is selfless and eternal. It endures all things and exists independently of the opinion of others. Love that is born in the soul and lives in the heart, will thrive and prosper in spite of the challenges it must face and the hardships it must endure.

Recipes for:

A Tale of Two Tabbies

Recipes from Kathi
Mini Cherry Cheesecakes
Strawberry Jell-O Salad
Strawberry Angel Cake
Boysenberry Bars

Recipes from Readers
Breakfast Bake—submitted by Joyce Aiken
Clam Pie—submitted by Nancy Farris
Taco Soup—submitted by Pam Curran
Grandma Meier's Potato Casserole—submitted by Vivian Shane
Peanut Butter Brownie Cake—submitted by Teri Fish
Mom's Gingersnaps—submitted by Pam Woodfield

Mini Cherry Cheesecakes

Preheat oven to 350 degrees.
Line cupcake pan with 12 liners.

Crust:
1½ cups graham cracker crumbs (or crushed cookie crumbs)
6 tbs. butter or margarine, melted
6 tbs. sugar

Mix together and fill bottom of 12 cupcakes.

Filling:
2 (8 oz.) pkgs. cream cheese, softened
¾ cup white granulated sugar
2 eggs
2 tbs. vanilla

Mix together until smooth and free of lumps. Divide between 12 cupcakes. Bake at 350 for 15 minutes or until set.

Let mini cheesecakes cool completely, then top with cherry pie (or other fruit) filling.

Strawberry Jell-O Salad

2 small boxes strawberry Jell-O
16 oz. (about 2 cups) sliced strawberries
1 cup chopped walnuts
16 oz. sour cream

Mix:
1 small box strawberry Jell-O (made per directions on box)
1 pt. (16 oz.) sliced strawberries
1 cup chopped walnuts (add more if you really like nuts)

Pour into bottom of 9 x 13 glass baking dish. Chill until set (about 2 hours).

After first layer is set:

Spread 16-oz. container of sour cream over the top (do not use low fat). Chill for 30 minutes.

Make second small box of strawberry Jell-O according to directions. Carefully pour or ladle the Jell-O on top of sour cream layer; be careful when placing this layer on top or you'll mess up the sour cream. Chill for 2 hours.

Strawberry Angel Cake

Make angel food cake according to directions on box; bake in angel flute cake pan. Cool completely. Cut top off about one-inch down. Scoop out middle, leaving adequate cake on sides.

Mix together:
1 small box strawberry Jell-O, made according to directions and chilled until set
⅓ small (8 oz.) Cool Whip
⅔ pint (16 oz.) fresh strawberries, cut up small

Fill cake with Jell-O mixture; there will be some mixture left in most cases. Replace cake "lid" that was set aside. Frost with remaining Cool Whip. Garnish with remaining whole strawberries.

Boysenberry Bars

Mix together:
2 cups flour
1½ cups long cooking oats
½ cup brown sugar, packed
1 cup butter (room temp.)

Reserve 1 cup of mixture. Press into greased 9 x 13 baking pan.

Cream together:
8 oz. cream cheese, softened
14 oz. can sweetened condensed milk
1 tsp. vanilla
1 pkg. (8 oz.) white chocolate chips

Spread over flour mixture.

Combine 1 can boysenberry pie filling (or any fruit). Mix with 2 tbs. cornstarch. Spread over cream cheese layer.

Sprinkle reserve flour mixture and 1 cup chopped salted cashew or peanuts over the top.

Bake at 375 degrees for 35 to 40 minutes or until golden.

Cool and cut into bars.

Breakfast Bake

Submitted by Joyce Aiken

1 can crescent dinner rolls
1 pkg. smoked ham (8 oz. Oscar Mayer), chopped
6 eggs
½ milk
½ tsp. pepper
1 cup shredded cheddar cheese
I cup shredded mozzarella cheese

Heat oven to 350 degrees. Unroll dough in 9 x 13 pan, firmly pressing holes and seams together to seal. Sprinkle ham over crust. Beat eggs, milk, and pepper with whisk until blended; pour over ham. Top with cheeses. Bake 25 minutes or until center is set.

Clam Pie

Submitted by Nancy Farris

This was one of best friend's go-to appetizers when I lived in Louisville, KY, back in the mid-eighties. I always think of her whenever I make it! Add a glass of white wine and you're set. I thought the clams went along with the Whales and Tails theme.

2–6 oz. cans chopped clams, undrained
Dash ground pepper
¾ cup seasoned Italian bread crumbs
1 stick unsalted butter, melted
Juice of ½ lemon
2 tsp. dried oregano
1 medium onion, chopped
American cheese slices
Parmesan cheese for top

Heat oven to 350 degrees.

Mix all of the above together, except for the cheeses. Pour into a buttered 8" casserole or pie plate. Make a lattice for the top by cutting the American cheese into ½ strips and arranging them on top. Sprinkle with Parmesan cheese.

Bake at 350 degrees for 30 minutes. Serve warm with crackers for dipping.

Taco Soup

Submitted by Pam Curran

This recipe came from a librarian I know from one of my previous schools. You get to know the librarian on staff quite well. It's a quick put-together soup and is delicious.

4 boneless chicken breasts
1 small white onion, chopped
1 can cream of mushroom soup
1 can cream of chicken soup
1 can Ro*tel tomatoes
1 can whole kernel corn
Morton seasoning salt
2 tbs. sugar
1 tsp. cumin
Tortilla chips

Dice chicken and onions and brown in a large pot. When the chicken is brown, add the soups, tomatoes, and corn. Add enough water to make a soup consistency. Season with the salt to taste. Add sugar and cumin. Allow the soup to simmer until the chicken and onions are completely cooked.

Serve over a bowl of tortilla chips. Serves approximately 16 one-cup servings.

You can make it lighter using the lighter version of the soups.

Grandma Meier's Potato Casserole

Submitted by Vivian Shane

This recipe has been in my family for several generations; the older recipes that get passed down always seem to taste better, even if the ingredients are nothing new!

2 lbs. frozen hash browns, thawed
½ cup melted margarine
1 tsp. salt
½ tsp. pepper
1 tbs. dried minced onion
1 can cream of chicken soup
1 pt. sour cream
2 cup grated cheddar cheese
1 large can Durkee French Fried Onions

Mix all ingredients except French fried onions and place in a 9 x 13 buttered baking dish. Top with French fried onions and bake at 350 degrees for 45–60 minutes.

Peanut Butter Brownie Cake

Submitted by Teri Fish

My grandma, Hazel Taylor, used to make this for my mom and aunt's birthdays and maybe one other time during the year. It brings back memories of my grandma and mom.

½ cup butter
1 cup sugar
2 eggs
1 tsp. vanilla
1 cup Hershey's Chocolate Syrup
1¼ cups unsifted flour
½ tsp. baking soda
1 cup peanut butter chips

Cream butter, sugar, eggs, and vanilla. Beat well. Add chocolate syrup and mix. Then add flour and baking soda and mix well. Mix in peanut butter chips. Pour into a greased 9 x 13 pan. Bake at 350 degrees for 30–35 minutes. Cool cake before frosting.

Frosting:

½ cup sugar
¼ cup canned milk
2 tbs. butter
1 cup peanut butter chips

1 tsp. vanilla

Combine sugar, canned milk, and butter into a small pan. Stir over medium heat until it comes to a full rolling boil. Remove from stove and quickly add peanut butter chips and stir until melted. Add vanilla and beat to a spreading consistency and frost cake.

Mom's Gingersnaps

Submitted by Pam Woodfield

This recipe was handed down from my grandmother, Ellen Shouldice, to my mother, Trish McGuire, in Canada, and now to me. Three generations so far.

¾ cup shortening
1 cup brown sugar
¼ cup Lyle's Golden Syrup molasses (or your favorite brand; dark corn syrup can also be substituted)
1 egg
1 cup raisins (more or less, depending on how much you like them)
2 cups all-purpose flour
1 tbs. ground ginger
2 tsp. baking soda
1 tsp. cinnamon
½ tsp. salt
 Granulated sugar to dip the cookies in.

Cream the shortening and brown sugar. Add the molasses, egg, and raisins and mix them together. Mix the dry ingredients together, then add to the creamed shortening and brown sugar mixture. Mix everything together well.

Roll cookie dough into a round ball about the size of a large marble. Sprinkle some granulated sugar on a plate or a piece of wax paper. Dip the top of the cookie ball in the sugar. (You can use a spoon and sprinkle it on the top if you prefer.) Place the cookie ball sugar side up on an ungreased cookie sheet.

Use two or three fingers on top of the cookie ball to push down and flatten it onto the cookie sheet. Repeat with the remainder of the batter.

Cook at about 350 degrees for 15 minutes until light brown. (Some ovens may require adjustment to a lower temperature and less cooking time.) Allow to cool and enjoy!

Makes about 3½ dozen cookies.

Books by Kathi Daley

Come for the murder,
Stay for the romance.

Zoe Donovan Cozy Mystery:

Halloween Hijinks
The Trouble With Turkeys
Christmas Crazy
Cupid's Curse
Big Bunny Bump-off
Beach Blanket Barbie
Maui Madness
Derby Divas
Haunted Hamlet
Turkeys, Tuxes, and Tabbies
Christmas Cozy
Alaskan Alliance
Matrimony Meltdown
Soul Surrender
Heavenly Honeymoon
Hopscotch Homicide
Ghostly Graveyard
Santa Sleuth
Shamrock Shenanigans

Zimmerman Academy Shorts

The New Normal
A New Beginning – *March 2016*

Paradise Lake Cozy Mystery:

Pumpkins in Paradise
Snowmen in Paradise
Bikinis in Paradise
Christmas in Paradise
Puppies in Paradise
Halloween in Paradise

Whales and Tails Cozy Mystery:

Romeow and Juliet
The Mad Catter
Grimm's Furry Tail
Much Ado About Felines
Legend of Tabby Hollow
Cat of Christmas Past
A Tale of Two Tabbies

Sand and Sea Hawaiian Mystery

Murder at Dolphin Bay – *March 2016*

Seacliff High Mystery:

The Secret
The Curse
The Relic

The Conspiracy
The Grudge

Road to Christmas
Romance:
Road to Christmas Past

Kathi Daley lives with her husband, kids, grandkids, and Bernese mountain dogs in beautiful Lake Tahoe. When she isn't writing, she likes to read (preferably at the beach or by the fire), cook (preferably something with chocolate or cheese), and garden (planting and planning, not weeding). She also enjoys spending time on the water when she's not hiking, biking, or snowshoeing the miles of desolate trails surrounding her home.

Kathi uses the mountain setting in which she lives, along with the animals (wild and domestic) that share her home, as inspiration for her cozy mysteries.

Kathi is a top 100 mystery writer on Amazon and won the 2014 award for both Best Cozy Mystery Author and Best Cozy Mystery Series.

She currently writes five series: Zoe Donovan Cozy Mysteries, Whales and Tails Mysteries, Tj Jensen Paradise Lake Mysteries, Sand and Sea Hawaiian Mysteries, and Seacliff High Teen Mysteries.

Stay up to date with her newsletter, *The Daley Weekly*.
http://eepurl.com/NRPDf

Kathi Daley Blog publishes each Friday
http://kathidaleyblog.com

Webpage www.kathidaley.com

Facebook at Kathi Daley Books -
www.facebook.com/kathidaleybooks

Kathi Daley Teen -
www.facebook.com/kathidaleyteen

Kathi Daley Books Group Page –
https://www.facebook.com/groups/569578823146850/

E-mail - kathidaley@kathidaley.com

Goodreads -
https://www.goodreads.com/author/show/7278377.Kathi_Daley

Twitter at Kathi Daley@kathidaley -
https://twitter.com/kathidaley

Amazon Author Page -
https://www.amazon.com/author/kathidaley

BookBub - https://www.bookbub.com/authors/kathi-daley

Pinterest - http://www.pinterest.com/kathidaley/

73472351R00130

Made in the USA
Lexington, KY
09 December 2017